B IS FOR BOSS'S BABY

OFFICE SECRETS - BOOK THREE

ANNIE J. ROSE

CHAPTER 1

NIK

"I'm not so sure about this guys," Toby said, looking nervous.

"What's not to be sure about?" Devin asked.

The conference room rivaled many of the most well-appointed offices in Manhattan. I wouldn't settle for anything less. Usually the long, dark-stained table running down the center of the room was lined on either side with expensive suits and intense stares, but on that day only two people were sitting across from me, which only exaggerated the differences between the two; the men were a study in contrasts. To the right was Devin McKay, polished, sophisticated, and self-assured; he was a serious mover and shaker in the financial world and exuded confidence. And to the left was Toby Michaels, he like an overgrown teenage nerd; Toby might have been a whiz with the software he designed and parlayed into a successful startup, but that wasn't doing him much good in our current situation.

In reality, he looked totally out of his element wading through the midst of the business negotiations. And that was exactly why I was there. The longer I sat in the conference room, the more I knew me being there was a good thing. My expertise was exactly what Toby's company needed. He was essentially flailing around without knowing what to do, and I was the ideal person to anchor him to the ground and help him reach his potential. Besides, the software he developed was the perfect fit for the application I had in my mind. This was a Captain Planet moment. With our powers combined, we could make a lot of money. Probably more money than Toby ever imagined making when he was tinkering around with the software.

I wasn't the only one who knew the potential of us coming together. Devin seemed to recognize the benefit of cooperation and was doing his best to talk it up to Toby. After ten years of knowing each other, Devin and I trusted each other and knew how to let each other do our thing. Right now, that meant sitting back and letting Devin do the talking. I sat back in my chair and watched him appeal to Toby and work on reeling him in. He talked up my successes and business prowess, trying to convince him it was in their best interest to team up with me. It was almost amusing listening to Devin rattle off the list of my accomplishments. He ticked them off with ease like he had memorized my entire curriculum vitae and the files for every one of my clients from the last few decades of me building my business, but it didn't yet have the effect Devin or I wanted.

Despite everything Devin told him, and the truly spectacular pep talk he'd unfurled since we met in the conference room, Toby remained hesitant. He wasn't totally convinced this was the move he wanted to make for his company. His green eyes flickered uncertainly back and forth between Devin and me.

"I'm worried about giving up control of my company,"

he finally admitted and that was my cue. Time to switch the approach and get me in on this conversation.

"Not at all. This will be a partnership in the truest sense of the world. This is not about me taking over or trying to force you out of what you have created. I know the work you've put into your company, but I also know the tremendous potential it carries. In this partnership, I will respect your input, and at the same time act as a mentor to you. As you've just heard from Devin, I have extensive experience building companies and turning them into successes. Think of me as your hype man. The years I have on you have allowed me to learn, take risks, make mistakes, and grow from those mistakes. I've developed a deep understanding of what it means to run a truly successful business positioned not just for immediate results, but in the long term.

"You now have the opportunity to benefit from all of that. Rather than being at the very beginning and having to try to get your foot in the door, I can give you a hand and help you climb up. You won't have to make the same mistakes I did. You won't have to deal with the same stumbling blocks or setbacks. My experience and skill are now yours, and I'll be here beside you to help you develop, strengthen, and hone your own."

Toby looked interested. I'd gotten his attention and some of my strategic words had burrowed their way into his thoughts. It was time to clinch.

"What we're offering you here isn't some flash-in-the-pan moment in the spotlight. We aren't interested in momentary success or fifteen minutes of fame, and I know you aren't either. You want to create something impactful. You want to build a future. You want to have the work you put in now pay off for years to come, and in ways you haven't yet thought up. We understand that and we want to help you achieve it. I give you my personal assurance everyone here will come out with more than agreeable profits."

Devin smiled widely. "Well, there you go. I personally see no downside to this proposition. Not every new business owner has someone like Nik willing to help them along. This is a huge opportunity, something that will propel your business in the right direction and ensure you stay on that path for years to come."

I held out my hands like I was showing there was nothing left on the table. "It really is the best of all worlds for both of us."

Toby stared at me for a few more seconds, processing what I'd said, then let his shoulders drop. I had him.

"All right," he said. "But I don't want a standard contract. The language in it needs to be very specific to preserve my authority in this as well."

I smiled and gave him a single, agreeing nod.

"Absolutely. I don't deal with standard contracts because there is no such thing as a standard agreement. Like I said, we are working together here to create the best situation for everybody involved. Of course, you will be able to review the contract thoroughly with your attorney before signing and bring up any concerns you may have with the language so it can be modified. I will personally go over it before giving to you to make sure it is acceptable," I said.

Standing, I extended my hand across the table. Toby stood and took it, finally cracking a smile as we shook on the fresh new deal. I gestured toward the door of the conference room and waited as they walked around the table so I could escort them out. Devin lagged slightly behind Toby, letting the younger man get ahead while he stayed back with me.

When Toby was far enough in front of us, Devin slapped me on the back and grinned.

"Well done, buddy. I look forward to making an obscene amount of money with you," he said.

I laughed. "Sounds good to me. Let's go get a drink to celebrate."

Devin and I had spent many a long night out together, divided between celebrations and drowning sorrows. The nights were heavier on the sorrows ten years before when I was going through my divorce. It had been a while since we'd gone out for a drink, but I figured this was as good an excuse as any. Devin shook his head.

"Can't. It sounds great and this is definitely something to celebrate, but I've got to get home. I've got a very pregnant wife at home, and she doesn't take kindly to me spending long nights at the bar."

I laughed and it was my turn to clap him on the back.

"Congrats, man. You get home and take care of her. Bring her some pickles and ice cream," I said.

Devin scoffed. "If only her cravings were that simple. Right now, she's on an Indian food kick, but only one dish, from one restaurant, from one part of the city."

"But you'll do it for her."

"Anytime, day or night," he confirmed.

"Then you better go so you can bring some home to her. We'll catch up soon," I told him.

After seeing Devin out of the building, I used my private elevator to return to my office. True to my word, I intended to make sure the partnership contract between my firm and Toby's company would be favorable. I didn't need to try to screw him out of anything or deceive him in any way. His software had the potential to be extremely valuable to me. Giving him a say and propping him up as the continued lead of his company didn't threaten that. Besides, the happier I kept him, the harder he would work to continue churning out development to increase our profits.

Sitting at my desk, I opened a document on my computer to start drafting out the bare bones of the partnership contract. When I was finished, I'd send them along to the legal department for fleshing out. A final read-through to ensure nothing significant was changed, and then they'd be off to Toby for the signature that would make the agreement official. I was excited about the new deal. By that point I was already a millionaire many times over, but that didn't quell my desire to achieve more. Landing this partnership could be just the thing I'd been looking for to push my empire to the next level.

The excitement had spiked my energy, and I didn't want to just let this milestone pass. I felt like celebrating, but not alone. Devin not being available disappointed me. We always had a good time together, but his excuse still had my thoughts reeling. A pregnant wife. I couldn't even imagine something like that or how it must have changed Devin's life. My company was the center of my existence. I'd never been able to pull myself away from work effectively enough to have a successful serious relationship. Just ask my ex-wife. That relationship was serious, possibly, but it sure as hell wasn't successful.

Devin must have been able to find that balance between his work and his home life I was never able to find. And he seemed incredibly happy about it. Maybe there really was something I was missing. Not that I would admit it to anyone, but I had started feeling lonely at times. Late at night when I got home and there was no one there to talk to about my day. On weekends when I sat at my desk rather than being out enjoying some activity or outing. When other people talked up their anticipation for their next vacation and came back with sunburns and phones brimming with pictures. Those were the moments I started thinking maybe all work and no play wasn't the way to live life. I worked my entire life to build the company and was proud of my accomplishments. My drive kept me pushing, never fully satisfied with anything because I knew there was always more. But recently, I started wondering if I wasn't going to be able to find that "more" putting in more hours at the office.

I forced myself to push the thoughts out of my mind and refocus on the contract in front of me. Wasting my energy on the negativity wasn't going to do me any good. Concentrating on the deal would give me all the excitement I needed for the time.

CHAPTER 2

JANE

"**D**ammit!"

I threw down my brush and let out an exasperated sound somewhere between a growl and a deep exhale. Raking my fingers back through my hair in a huff, I glared at the canvas in front of me. It wasn't turning out as planned. I could almost trace exactly when it all went to hell. My change in emotion completely threw off the painting. The entire thing was ruined. Standing up from the stool positioned in front of my easel, I abandoned the canvas. I stormed out of my workspace and toward the kitchen. I loved the large, airy space I'd carved out of my house and turned into my own little haven for art. It was where I could crawl through my thoughts and translate them into reality with the touch of my brush, but that day, it wasn't the refuge I wanted it to be.

The painting was a mess, and it was an apparent wreck that managed to show everything I'd been trying not to show. I walked up to the sink and shoved the handle of the faucet, so a stream of water rushed out into the porcelain enamel-coated basin. It took a few seconds for the water to heat enough for me to push my hands into it.

"Everything is just completely fucked-up," I muttered to myself. "I don't know why I thought it was going to be any different. I should have known it wasn't going to come out the way I wanted. Fucked-up input and fucked-up painting that's my new mantra. I'm going to cross-stitch it into a damn sampler."

Paint rinsed from my arms and hands and slipped across the white surface of the sink. It blended into murky gray as it swirled down the drain. Pumping soap into my palm, I lathered my skin to wash away the rest of the paint, and then rinsed. Just as I was drying my hands, my phone buzzed in the pocket of my smock. I tossed the towel aside and grabbed my phone out, glancing at the screen. It was my best friend, Elly. Thank god. Exactly who I needed to talk to in that moment. As if just seeing her name opened some sort of valve inside me and released the flood gates, I answered the call without bothering to greet her.

"You will not believe how completely screwed up today has been. I'm talking straight out of last century, fucking Hallmark Channel movie screwed up," I said.

"Hello to you, too. What the hell happened?" Elly asked.

I drew in a breath and launched into a recitation of the morning's events, my energy bordering on panic. Even as I told her what happened, I could see it playing out in my mind. The pristine setting of my parents' Upper West Side mansion only made the warped situation worse.

"My parents invited me over for brunch. They didn't say anything or prepare me for what was coming. Nothing. Just 'come over for brunch.' So, I'm sitting there with them eating crepes and eyeing the quiche when they let the hammer drop. They've decided it's time for me to get married. Just like that. It wasn't a suggestion or an idea, like they were wondering what my life plans are or anything. It was just them informing me, 'Jane, we've decided the time has come for you to marry.'"

"Did you tell them you're not dating anyone?" Elly asked.

"Elly, you know my parents. Do you honestly think they would dive into a conversation like that without having a plan? They don't care I don't have a boyfriend. They wouldn't care if I *did* have one. It doesn't change anything for them. Not only have they decided I need to get married, but they've also decided *who* I'm going to marry," I told her.

There was a beat while I let that sink in for her.

"What?" she finally asked.

"Yeah. This wasn't just a check-in about my life and them letting me know that at twenty-seven years old, I am clearly creeping right up on my expiration date. This was a full-blown arranged marriage announcement."

"And who's the lucky guy?" Elly quipped.

"Preston fucking Howell," I spat.

The image of the son of my parents' very close friends, the Howells, formed in my mind. I couldn't believe my mother and father had gotten it into their minds he would be the one they decided to pair me off with. Not that it was all that unexpected in the greater scheme of things. If they were going to go medieval on my love life and start offering me up to families, the Howells were going to be their first choice. And Preston always did seem to them like a built-in match for their free-spirited, redheaded daughter.

"As in the boy next door?" Elly asked, sounding shocked.

"Not exactly. That would almost be cute. The Howell

mansion is two blocks over and one block up."

"How silly of me. Practically from different worlds," she teased.

"Actually, not at all that's what got us to this point. I've known Preston Howell most of my life. Ever since my parents and his became friends, we've been pushed together at various points. Events, parties, even a few ill-advised family vacations. And, of course, they were always chittering and whispering behind their cocktails about how cute we were together. I assure you, we were anything but cute together," I told her.

"How well do you know him?" Elly asked. "I know you've known him for a long time, but were you ever close?"

"No. It's impossible to be close with Preston Howel, but I do know him well enough to know he is not only the epitome of a spoiled rotten brat but a boring douche as well. He's the type of guy that is the absolute reason people hate rich kids. We're not even kids anymore, and he can still make people hate rich kids. He's an entitled ass who thinks the world owes him everything because his last name is Howell. The very idea of work is repulsive to him. Like it offends his delicate sensibilities to even consider having a job or putting any effort into life. He believes everything should simply be handed to him and there is no benefit to effort, ambition, striving for anything, or earning even a little bit of his way in the world."

"So, I'm assuming you didn't gleefully jump at the chance for them to present you at a formal betrothal?" Elly asked.

I almost laughed. At least Elly could take a little of the edge off.

"No," I said. "I most certainly didn't. There's no way in living hell I would ever agree to marry him."

"How did they react to that?"

"Beyond mad," I said. "They were furious that I wouldn't even consider it. They wanted me to take my time and really think it all the way through. My mother even went and got a pad of paper and pen so I could write out a pro and con list. She seriously thought if I just took some time to sit there and look at the situation from their perspective, I would come to the same conclusion as them because that's exactly how you should go into an engagement. A list. Maybe we could get really sexy and throw a pie chart in there."

I let out a sigh and leaned back against the counter.

"Is it safe to assume you didn't go through with the pro-and-con list?" Elly asked.

"Yes, it is. I figured it wouldn't be productive to write 'con: he's an arrogant, self-absorbed, dull-as-toast prick, and I'd end up choking myself with his Prada tie before our wedding night was over. Pro: if I agree to marry him and then get into a horrific accident that robs me of my looks, senses, faculties, and functionality, he would still be obligated to me.'"

"Yeah, that probably wouldn't have gone over too well," she agreed.

"As it is, my fairly adamant refusal to even talk the situation through didn't go over too well," I informed her.

"What happened?"

"They threatened to cut me off financially if I didn't agree to marry Preston."

"Well, shit," she said.

"Shit, indeed. So, I did what any sophisticated, worldly, self-respecting woman of means would do in a situation like this. I flung myself dramatically onto the chaise lounge in the living room and declared I would rather starve in the streets as an artist than marry the likes of Preston Howell," I said.

"Wooooooooo! That a girl! Way to stick it to the man." Elly suddenly sounded like she was several feet away, and there was an enthusiastic round of applause, which meant she likely put me on speakerphone. I could only hope she wasn't somewhere public where other people were listening in on my life crisis. "I am so proud of you for standing up to your parents. I know that had to be hard for you, but, seriously, what are you really going to do, because starving doesn't sound like much fun."

The sudden shift in her tone made me sigh. She was right. Starving in the streets had a certain romantic ring to it, and I was sure I'd be immortalized in a full range of folk mediums from chalk drawings on the sidewalk to songs sung around the firepit, but that wasn't exactly what I had in mind when I looked into my future.

"I don't really know," I admitted. "But I think it likely involves getting a job."

"Like a job, job? A real job?" Elly asked.

It was a legitimate question.

"Yes. Only, I'm not sure exactly how to go about doing that. I've never had a job before. I don't know where to start," I said.

"Don't worry. I've had jobs before. I promise I will help you. In fact..." Her voice trailed off, and I could almost see the smile stretching across her freckle-sprinkled face. "I might have a lead on a job you would be perfect for, considering your art background."

She filled me in on the position with the marketing department she'd learned about through her husband, Devin. It sounded like an amazing opportunity, but nerves made me hesitant.

"I'm afraid I won't know what to do when I get there. Do I clock in? Is that still a thing? Do people still do that? Like on a big time clock? I saw that in a movie once," I said.

"Was that movie *Nine to Five*?" she laughed. "Just calm down. You're going to be okay. Everything is going to be just fine. You are strong and smart and resourceful and creative, and when I've gone through enough adjectives to make you feel better about the whole situation, just let me know."

I laughed. "I think I'm good."

"Okay. You are. You are good, and you're going to be even better. You're taking control of your life, and it's going to be fine," she said.

"Thank you, Elly."

The call ended and I held my phone to my chest, going over the conversation in my head. My thoughts then drifted back to my brunch with my parents and the showdown over my future. I wondered if I was really making the right decision. I had always been wealthy. I was born into an affluent family and raised in the bubble of wealth. I'd always had whatever I wanted without even thinking about it. As much as I vilified Preston for being disconnected and entitled, a little voice in the back of my head said I wasn't too far off from him. The only thing I'd ever had to work for in my life was my art, and that was completely different. Everything I truly needed, anything I wanted, was right there for me without a second thought. The prospect of all that changing was scary.

But the alternative was much worse. Being Mrs. Preston Howell wasn't something I could even begin to wrap my brain around. Even if it meant a life of luxury and continuing to never have to want for or worry about anything, it wasn't worth throwing my future, me, away for. It was time for me to grow up, get a job, and take care of myself.

CHAPTER 3

The office I was using was definitely not what I was accustomed to. My current surroundings were a snapshot of the distinct differences between Toby Michaels and me as people and as businessmen. While I leaned toward the sophistication and luxury of dark wood, leather, and strong accents, Toby's style was sleek and inspired by the technology he loved. Desks were clear acrylic, chairs slopes of ergonomic fabric. Yoga balls tucked into metal hoops with legs sat in the corners of the offices to offer an alternative to the more conventional chairs. It was bright, airy, and had an energy that managed to feel simultaneously fast and laid-back. I could only imagine what the company was going to be like when we cultivated it to the point of needing even more employees.

It wasn't my style, but if it fit Toby, then it didn't really matter if it fit me. I wasn't there to take over and change his company. I was there to turn it into something incredible that would benefit both of us in spades. And to do that I needed to have space to do it, so I commandeered an office where I could hold the meetings I needed. And that morning it was with Ethan, the marketing director, and his assistant, Maddie.

"Branding is critical," I told them. "If this company is going to break through and stand out against the competition, it's going to be all about recognition and appeal. Everyone has a brand these days. You're nothing without one, and we need to find Toby's."

"I completely agree," Ethan said. "It's not enough to present the quality of the software or the benefits it can offer to the consumer. We have to find a way to make the company appeal to the consumer as a part of their daily life. It needs to be immediately recognizable and reliable."

"Yes," I said, pointing at him with the tip of my pen. "Reliable. Too many companies these days are trying to refresh or reinvent themselves and appeal to all sorts of different demographics, depending on what they think at any given moment. It can give them little bursts of relevance, but in the end, it makes them look shaky and like they're trying too hard as if they don't know themselves. We need to make sure this company looks strong, secure, and fully established within the brand. Toby has been trying to get this thing off the ground for a few years now, so we need to come at this from a couple different angles."

"What do you mean?" Maddie asked.

"With enough of a push, Toby can burst out onto the scene like a dynamic, exciting new company, and we want to capitalize on that fresh energy. At the same time, the company has been around for a while. We don't want to pretend that time doesn't exist. It's all about leveraging the experience while demonstrating new initiative and commitment to staying on the cutting edge. We want the consumers to appreciate the fresh perspective and also the grounded knowledge. Getting the brand out there and getting it noticed is key," I told them.

"That sounds great," Ethan said. "I'd like to show you some of the things we've been working on if you'll come with us to the marketing department. There are some preliminary sketches and a few ideas we can develop."

"Absolutely. Let's go," I said.

Ethan and Maddie walked with me to the marketing department and led me into Ethan's office where several large storyboards sat on the desk. He picked up the first and offered it over to me. I glanced at it, nodded, and reached for the second.

"They're just a few ideas. Some initial concepts to go on," the marketing director said.

I looked over the rest of the sketches, then went back to the first and looked over them all again. They were actually very good, much better than I was anticipating.

"I'm impressed," I told them. "These are good. They are more artistic than I'm used to seeing, especially at this stage of the development."

Maddie grinned. "I'll bring in the artist. She's a new employee but has incredible talent."

She left, and a few moments later returned. I glanced up and was struck by the woman beside her. The artist was stunningly beautiful, and I couldn't take my eyes off her for several long seconds. Impeccably dressed and elegantly groomed, she was the picture of professionalism, far more polished than I expected for an artist. Now I was even more impressed, but for completely different reasons.

"This is Jane. She's the newest employee in the marketing department. Jane, this is Nik Nygard. He's the head of the company we merged with," Maddie explained.

Jane nodded and held out one graceful, perfectly manicured hand.

"It's nice to meet you, Mr. Nygard," she said.

Her voice made my stomach tighten, and the smooth softness of her hand in mine made me want to feel much more of her skin. My instant attraction to her surprised me.

"Good to meet you, Jane," I said, forcing away the thoughts and hoping my reaction to her wasn't obvious in my voice. "I really like your sketches. They're high quality, and your ideas are great. Now it's just a matter of streamlining them into a marketable approach. We need to maximize the impact of the campaign by utilizing all available channels. The design we choose has to be readily translatable into a variety of mediums. Social media, print, billboards, live marketing events, merchandising, content media. We need to take the idea and turn it into something consumers will instantly recognize and link directly back to the company's mission."

I continued talking strategy with Ethan, expecting Jane to jump in with thoughts or ideas, but she didn't. Instead, she stood still beside Maddie, starting at us with widened eyes. Sometimes her head switched back and forth as if our conversation was a tennis match and she was trying to keep up. Remembering Maddie introducing her as a new employee, I decided to give her the benefit of the doubt. She might have just been nervous about her first big project or intimidated by me. It wouldn't have been the first time either of those things had happened when I was working with a new company or even an established company. She could just need a bit of a push to nudge her in the right direction.

"What do you think, Jane?" I asked.

Her wide brown eyes flashed to me, and soft, full lips parted slightly before she shook her head.

"I'm sorry, what?" she asked.

Frustration started to build inside me, and I drew in a breath to calm it down.

"Ethan and I were discussing the feasibility of translating these images into marketable merchandise. Establishing the brand as already desirable as a lifestyle will enhance the credibility and entrench the company into conversation and ongoing social transactions," I said.

Color splashed on Jane's cheeks, and it was obvious she was struggling to come up with something to say. The frustration peaked, churning in my chest. This campaign had to go perfectly, and though Jane's sketches demonstrated she was talented, she was very clearly out of her league.

"Thank you, Jane, Maddie. If you'll excuse me, I have a few things to discuss with Ethan," I said.

The women exchanged glances, and Maddie looked to Ethan, but he wouldn't make eye contact with her. They walked out of the office, slowly closing the door behind them. When we were alone, I looked at Ethan.

"That was worrisome," I told him.

"You don't like the ideas for developing the campaign?" Ethan asked.

"No, the ideas are great. The problem is Jane didn't give any of them. She didn't have anything to say in the conversation at all. I have to admit it concerns me that she doesn't seem to know what's going on. She's obviously a very talented artist, but she doesn't seem to know what she's doing from a marketing standpoint. The quality of this campaign is critical, and I'm concerned she's not in her element here," I pointed out.

Ethan nodded. "I have similar doubts. She doesn't come

with work experience or any references to support her abilities, but she was highly recommended, and Maddie has promised to go over her work and mentor her in this new position. I trust Maddie completely and know the caliber of her work. She will be able to help Jane reach the level she needs to be at."

"That needs to happen immediately. We don't have the time, and frankly, I don't have the patience to babysit someone who doesn't know what they are doing or participate in a summer enrichment program. I need the utmost professionalism and skill. We can't afford any mistakes. If something goes wrong, I will hold you personally responsible for choosing the wrong team."

One hand still gripping the storyboard in front of him, Ethan swallowed hard. I'd made my point. I waited, giving him the opportunity to respond, but he didn't. Taking his silence as an assurance he wouldn't let the project fail and would see to it Maddie trained Jane properly, I headed out of the marketing department. I walked directly into Toby's office, and he looked up from his desk at me and smiled.

"How are things going?" he asked.

I decided to skirt around the question rather than answering it directly. Now wasn't the time to tell Toby about Jane or my hesitation. Ethan assured me Maddie would whip her into shape and make her an asset to the team, and I was going to give him the benefit of the doubt. At this point, he had little choice but to make sure he made good on that promise. Toby trusted my insights into the staffing structure of his company, and he would listen to my opinions regarding the performance of anyone working for him. Especially someone in a directorship role within a department as vitally important to the ongoing success of his business as marketing. Because of that, Ethan knew his future with the company, or at least his position within the hierarchy, hung in the balance.

"We got a lot done. I went to the marketing department and went over some of the preliminary plans for branding and getting your company out in front of the consumers," I told him. "I'm actually going to head back to my main office to take care of a few things, but there's still a lot more to be done so I'll be back later," I told him.

"Sounds good," Toby said.

I gave him a wave and left the building. All the way back to my own office, I couldn't get the thoughts of Jane out of my head. Even when I arrived back and shut myself behind my heavy door and sat at my dark wood desk to look into a few other projects, her face wouldn't leave my thoughts. When it wasn't her face, it was her body that dominated my mind. No matter what paperwork, emails, or other tasks I tried to force myself to think about, increasingly naughty thoughts took over. I couldn't stop thinking about the sweet, musky scent of her perfume and how velvety her skin looked. She was so beautiful, even if she didn't know what she was doing.

I forced myself to stop thinking about her and focus. I had to get this work done and get back to Toby's office to keep chipping away at everything that needed to be done to build his company and prepare it for true launch. The marketing campaign was just one piece of making sure it was ready to present to what could often be ruthless, judgmental consumers that needed to be my concentration. Regardless of how gorgeous and sexy she was, Jane was a distraction I didn't need at that moment.

"Way to go Jane," I scolded my reflection. "Could you have been any more useless in there?"

I pressed both hands to the side of the bathroom sink and hung my head forward, drawing in a deep breath. I held it in for a few seconds, then let it out slowly. It didn't do much to calm me down, so I turned on the faucet and splashed a handful of cold water onto my face. It hit me before I thought of its impact on my makeup. Fortunately, I tended to lean toward waterproof makeup on a regular basis. It didn't require as many touch-ups and gave me a bit of an insurance policy in the event I was caught in a sudden rainstorm, or got called out for my complete lack of experience and knowledge by my gorgeous new boss.

Letting out a deep sigh, I closed my eyes and tried to catch my breath. Meeting Nik Nygard was almost a blur. When Maddie came in and told me to come with her, she said I was going to get to meet the new boss, and she sounded so excited about it. I thought I was heading in to find a brainstorming session or even was going to get praised for my hard work. Meeting him was so much tougher than I ever would have thought. He was nothing like what I imagined he was going to be. Thinking about someone with as much influence as him, I imagined someone stuffy and boring. Someone like my father. I wasn't expecting somebody as handsome as he was. And he was certainly handsome. Incredibly attractive, powerful, and direct, he dominated the entire space of the office. It was like he took up more space than anyone else there, and even though Ethan and Maddie were with us, neither of them really registered. It was all about Nik.

Unfortunately, it wasn't exactly the pep talk and pat on the back I was hoping for. He liked my work. He was impressed by my sketches, which was nice to hear, but the positivity pretty much ended there. When he and Ethan launched into their conversation about marketing strategy and branding methods, I quickly got left behind. They rattled off terms and debated the benefits of theories and concepts I couldn't even begin to offer any input about. The few questions he'd asked me left me stumbling, and I was sure I said something I would be humiliated by once it ran back through my head. Nik clearly wasn't impressed by my failed answers, and I was terrified of getting fired. I mean that would be my luck. Landing my very first job and promptly losing it because I couldn't keep up.

But it wasn't just the thought of getting fired that sent a chill of trepidation through me. I was also afraid of just how attracted I was to the very man I assumed would be doing the firing.

Behind me, the bathroom door opened. There was a brief moment of sheer horror where my mind gave the illogical jump to thinking Nik was storming the ladies' room purely for the purpose of giving me the boot. It was ridiculous, but a wave of relief still washed over me when I looked into the mirror and saw Maddie's face reflected back toward me. My shoulders dropped slightly, and I glanced over my shoulder at her. Her face twisted up in concern, and her eyebrows knitted together as she stepped across the bathroom to put a comforting hand on my back.

"It's all right," she comforted me. "That went really well."

I gave her an incredulous look.

"Are you serious?" I asked. "Were you in the same meeting I was? He thinks I'm a complete idiot."

"No, he doesn't."

She shook her head and did her best to try to seem convincing, but I could see the concern in her eyes. The bathroom had great lighting and a flattering mirror, but it couldn't cover up the effects of that disaster.

"Yes, he absolutely does. Did you see the way he looked at me when he and Ethan started talking about all that stuff and I had no idea what was going on? He really liked my sketches and all, but I couldn't keep up with the conversation and didn't know what they were talking about. By the end there it was almost like he was asking me questions and staring at me to see just how much I could manage to humiliate myself in the span of ten minutes. He's going to toss my ass right out into the parking lot as soon as I walk out of here," I said.

"No, he's not," Maddie said. "I know for a fact he is not going to fire you as soon as you walk out of here."

I looked at her hopefully. "Really? How do you know that?"

"Because I just watched him leave. He's not going to be here when you walk out of the bathroom," she said, then smiled.

I let out a sound somewhere between a laugh and an exhale and shook my head.

"Perfect. He was so disappointed and exasperated by me he couldn't even bear to stay in the same building as I am."

Maddie laughed. "I really don't think it's like that. Ethan didn't say anything to me about Nik wanting to fire you. He just emphasized that we need to work together to get you up to speed. And that's perfectly fine. I told you from the beginning I would mentor you and make sure you knew everything you needed to know. I'll help you learn about all the marketing lingo and the different approaches they were talking about. You just keep coming up with awesome ideas and making those amazing sketches. I believe in you and your natural talent."

"You do?" I asked.

"Absolutely. I believed in you from the first moment Elly introduced us and I saw your sketches. This is something you were just meant to do that doesn't mean it's going to be easy. You'll have to work fast and hard to get all this under your belt and prove yourself to Ethan and to Nik."

"I will. I promise I will work as hard as I possibly can. This is the only shot I have, and I can't blow it," I told her.

"You won't. I won't let you. Not just because if your ass gets tossed out into the parking lot, mine goes right along with it," Maddie said.

I laughed and she wrapped an arm around my shoulders, giving me an encouraging squeeze. It felt good to know I had a friend at the office, someone who would see me through and help me succeed rather than being in competition against me.

Not taking a lunch break that day meant I could leave early without anyone really noticing. Maddie assured me we'd start the next day and told me to go home and get some rest. And that's exactly what I wanted to do, but it wasn't so easy. There really wasn't a home to go back to. I returned to what used to be my home, a spacious loft apartment I'd meticulously decorated and adored. It was all packed up then. I sold most of the furniture to build up a little nest egg to help smooth the transition from "pampered rich girl" to "scrappy working girl." Unfortunately, it wasn't feeling so much like a smooth transition as it was survival. There were a few more things left out from my last night there. I was packing them up into one last duffle bag to bring over to my new, much smaller apartment when the elevator buzzed.

I opened my door and saw Preston Howell step out of the elevator. Resisting the urge to roll my eyes and close the door in his face, I interrupted him before he could speak instead.

"What are you doing here, Preston?" I asked.

"I come on behalf of both our parents," he said, taking a step toward me. "I would like you to reconsider your decision and give me a chance."

He spoke with all the romance and poetry of reading charges at traffic court.

"We have nothing in common. We don't like any of the same things, we don't have any similar hobbies or aspirations," I pointed out.

"So, we find some things to share," he said. "It really can't be that difficult."

"That's the thing," I said. "It shouldn't be that difficult, but it would be. We have no idea what it would be like to attempt to have a relationship like that because we've never even dated. We don't spend time together, we've never even shared a meal just the two of us, and you expect that to be the bedrock of a successful marriage?"

"I'm willing to work on it if you are."

There was no energy in the words. This was playing out like one of those schlocky romance movies shown late at night on women's networks and that I secretly devoured. Only, in one of those movies this would be the moment when Preston would suddenly discover the spark of warmth and humanity inside him. He'd develop actual emotion and make an impassioned plea for me to change my mind and give him the chance to show me the man he could be. Instead, he looked at me like I was number four on his to-do list for the day and he was ready to check me off and move on to his evening deep-tissue massage.

Instead, he was just pissing me off.

"That's great, Preston, but I'm not. I know it's comforting to you, but I'm not going to let my parents dictate every minute detail of my life. I'm taking control of my future and living the life I want to. I recommend you grow a pair and try it too."

Slinging my duffle bag over my shoulder and shutting the door behind me, I walked past Preston. I didn't know how long he stood there in the hallway, probably processing what it meant for someone to actually say no to him, but he wasn't there by the time I hailed a cab and climbed into the back seat. I directed the driver to my new apartment and let my head fall back against the seat as I let out a heavy breath.

I had either forgotten what the tiny new apartment looked like, or my brain had gone into self-preservation mode and was trying to protect me by blocking it out. Either way, when I managed to wrestle the door open and step inside, the reality of the surroundings hit me hard. All my belongings I had left were crammed into the cramped space. Each of the small handful of rooms was filled to the brim, and I had the distinct impression there wasn't even room in there for me.

By the ominous way some of the stacks of boxes leaned as I wove my way through the narrow path into the bedroom, it seemed my stuff might share the sentiment. Finally, I got to the bedroom and dropped down onto the bed. Looking around at my new reality, I reminded myself I could do this. Millions of other people had jobs and took care of themselves. A lot of people did it straight out of high school and without the kinds of connections I had. Every day people went out into the world, got jobs, earned money, and made their own way. They paid for their own places to live, they figured out paying bills, and they made it. How hard could it be?

Well, screw my optimism and my ambition. The universe seemed to think I had much more of a lesson to learn.

No sooner had the question gone through my mind than I heard a telltale sizzle and pop, and all the lights in my apartment went out. Even the fuse box didn't believe in me. Sitting alone in the dark, I let out a sigh.

CHAPTER 5

NIK

A few days after meeting with Ethan about the branding campaign team, work hadn't slowed down. I was still staying late at the office every night, burning the midnight oil to ensure we didn't lose momentum on any of the projects we were already doing. My main focus for my involvement in the merger with Toby's company was the marketing, but there were many other things to do to get him ready. There was a reason he hadn't been able to get traction and make himself a success yet, not that he was unskilled or didn't have what it took to find that success. He absolutely did have it. He just needed somebody to find and cultivate it that's why I was there. Now that I had skin in the game, I was relentless to squeeze every bit of potential out of the business and maximize the benefit of his existing software and anything else he developed, but that made for long nights and intense work. I didn't mind it. I was accustomed to hard work and having projects that were important consume me. Especially in the early stages when things were still finding their rhythm and so much could go so wrong, so quickly. I wasn't going to let that happen.

But it was nights like that when the loneliness started creeping into the edges of my mind. Being alone in the office was a much more isolating and intense feeling of being alone than if I was at home. There being alone was normal. Ten years gone from my divorce, and I was used to living alone. The vast majority of the time I was able to convince myself I preferred it that way, too. It meant when I finally did manage to pry myself away from work and get home, I could really relax. I didn't have to worry about what I was walking into or if there would be something to stop me from pouring a drink and losing myself in mindless TV before I went to bed. I knew what it was like for that to not be an option.

Being at the office, though, was different. The silent and darkened offices were just a reminder of all the people who should have been there. While I didn't interact with most of the people who went to the office, being there completely by myself did sometimes make my mind drift to the sense of loneliness I tried to ignore. I mean, I wasn't a complete recluse, and I did enjoy the company of women from time to time, but even that didn't fill the void.

I'd been staring at the same projections for over an hour, and my eyes were starting to burn. I needed a cup of coffee to push me over the wall. No secretaries or errand runners were available to do that particular task for me, so I pushed back from the desk and headed toward the break room. The rush of the coffee maker filled the silence, and seconds later started filling the mug I shoved in place, but I heard something I was sure wasn't the burbling of the coffee. It sounded like a voice. Not just a voice—a seriously pissed-off voice swearing at something down the hall. It definitely wasn't what I was expecting to hear in an office I assumed was empty except for me. But since it was the high voice of a woman and she seemed more frustrated than angry or afraid, I wasn't too concerned.

Curiosity brought me down the hallway toward the copy room, where I was sure the voice originated. A glance inside proved me right. And also made my eyes roll so hard there was a risk of me tipping over backward. Jane was inside, struggling with the copier and seemingly deep in an argument with it.

Did this woman seriously have no experience?

"Having trouble?" I asked.

Jane jumped at the interruption, her head snapping over to look at me. A fierce blush rose to her cheeks and splashed across her pale chest. Usually a reaction like that would aggravate me even more. For som e reason in Jane, it aroused me. My mind lit up and my body ignited, instantly reacting to her. What the hell was it about this woman that lit me on fire in a matter of seconds? It was most certainly not her basic office skills. Those just didn't seem to exist.

Jane looked embarrassed and stumbled over words for a few seconds before she gave up trying to give me any explanation. She turned her attention to trying to gather up the papers strewn around the room. Either she'd had one hell of a temper tantrum and threw a handful of papers up in the air in exasperation, or the machine had malfunctioned. Considering her muttering and creative streams of profanity, I strongly considered the possibility it was a little of both. The copy machine made a sound I'd never heard before and sounded akin to a death rattle. That definitely wasn't normal.

I rushed forward and took over. Looking over the

machine, I identified the paper jam and fixed it easily. Re-setting the machine, I reached my hand toward her.

"Come here," I said, a little gruffer than I perhaps intended. "Let me show you how to actually work this thing. Have you ever used a copier before?"

Jane shook her head as she walked over unprotestingly in my grip and stared down at the copy machine like it was some sort of beast I beat into submission but could rise up again at any second.

"No," she told me. "To be honest with you, I don't exactly have a ton of office experience."

"I gathered that," I told her. "All right, when you want to make a copy, you press this button."

She stepped up close to me as I led her through the steps of making copies. I could smell her perfume, and when she leaned slightly forward to make sure she could see everything, she brushed against me just enough to leave a trail of heat across my skin. Being that close to her was intoxicating, and I had to restrain myself from trying to kiss her. My mouth tingled with the want of her. I leaned my head toward her, just wanting to be further in her orbit. There was something about the woman I couldn't get enough of.

"All right, I think I've got it," she said after I went through the process with her twice.

"Do you want me to run a couple through for you?" I asked.

Jane looked over at me, and the tip of her tongue just barely grazed her bottom lip. It was everything I could do not to chase it with my own.

"Sure," she said.

I took the first page she handed me and looked down at it. The image was beautiful. I made the copies, then moved on to the next. She didn't stop me from taking over making the copies, and as I continued, the images drew me in further and further. I was entranced. After examining one of the images for several seconds, I realized Jane was staring at me. I held up the drawing.

"I really like what I see," I told her.

"Really?" she asked.

"These are really amazing. They're exactly what I imagined for the campaign," I told her.

She gave a modest half shrug and glanced down at the image with me.

"They're just a few of the sketches I've done for the branding campaign. Maddie walked me through everything you and Ethan were talking about, and I used my understanding of it to come up with these and a few others," she said.

"There are others?" I asked, my interest definitely piqued.

"Yes," she said.

"I want to see the rest of them."

Jane looked decidedly alarmed by the announcement and opened her mouth like she was going to say something. When no protest came out, she finally closed her mouth and nodded. I finished making the copies and then followed her out of the copy room. She led me through the halls to the marketing department and a small office. The holder for the name plaque on the door was empty, and a piece of paper was taped to the doorframe with her name on it. It had a temporary, tenuous feeling to it I'm sure made her feel somewhat on edge every time she saw it.

She brought me into the office and gestured at the desk. Several other sketches spread across the top showed a full range of thoughts and approaches. It was as if Jane had managed to look inside my mind and capture exactly what I wanted out of the campaign. She didn't know much about marketing and was woefully unprepared for the mechanical challenges of such simple tasks as making copies, but there was something about her. Somehow, she managed to capture the heart of the marketing angle for the new app without me even having to spell it out for her.

"This is incredible," I told her. "I don't know how you did it, but you got exactly what I wanted."

"I did?" she asked. "I was expecting Maddie to show them to you and then come back with rounds of revisions and changes you wanted in order to get them anywhere near close to your vision."

"Honestly, so was I," I admitted. "After our meeting the other day, I knew you had the artistic ability to create the visual I was looking for, but I didn't have a tremendous amount of confidence you were going to be able to internalize what I was going for and translate it into the art without a lot of specific guidance."

She shot me a glare.

"Thanks," she said sarcastically.

I didn't try to backpedal or reassure her. There was no reason to. Coddling her wasn't going to benefit her, just like it didn't for anyone else. Being straightforward and clear was the only way to get through to people and demand quality work.

"Somehow, you managed to do it, though. There are nuances to the marketing approach I wanted but couldn't figure out exactly how to say it. Yet, you captured them. These sketches are like you put my exact thoughts onto paper, only more exceptional, more beautiful. It's remarkable, and I'm beyond impressed," I said.

Her complete lack of knowledge had frustrated and

concerned me at first. I was convinced there would be no way she could live up to my expectations and worried she would drag the campaign down. Despite Ethan's reassurances and Maddie being there to train her along, Jane seemed close to a liability. Now it was almost like her not being as knowledgeable and experienced as the rest of the team was a benefit. Maybe getting too wrapped up in the technical elements and specific, detailed strategy would have restricted her. She wouldn't have been able to let her creativity fully flow and may not have been able to create the perfection she had.

I looked up and she glanced over at me. Our eyes met and I felt the wide, light brown pools draw me in. I never wanted to look away from them. A strand of her long, red hair slipped out of the clip that held some of it back and fell down the curve of her face. Time stopped, and for a moment I was barely even breathing. She was the only thing I saw, the only thing I wanted to see. I wanted her. Badly. And it wasn't just for her talent. I wanted to take her into my arms and bring her close to my body. I wanted to feel her skin against mine and count her heartbeats on my chest. I wanted to hold her, to touch and explore every inch of her, to taste her. Jane was unlike any woman I'd ever encountered, and I craved her. Just being there with her wouldn't be enough. I needed more, even if I knew it wasn't what I should let myself want.

I couldn't even believe what was happening. If I was one for superstition and hadn't had more than my fair share of lucid dreams in my life, I might have wanted to ask the universe to pinch me.

Fuck it. Pinch me. It was really that unbelievable. I was reeling from my good fortune and almost afraid to breathe. I was so worried it was going to go away if I made one little move. Somehow, out of what could possibly be a miracle, I managed to impress my boss. And not just impressed him in the way I did when he first saw my sketches and thought they were good. This was even better than that. I impressed him after totally humiliating myself and thinking he was going to ball me up and trash me like last week's takeout menus. This was redemption admiration, and I couldn't get enough of it.

"The way you managed to make the logo look both fresh and classic is exceptional. Technology is really exciting to a lot of people, but some are still wary of it. We don't want to alienate potential consumers by making them feel out of the loop or like they aren't relevant just by looking at the marketing. You created something that ensures that won't happen. It's wonderful," he said.

I was glowing. It was like his words opened up the skies and the warmth of the sun was shining down on me. For the first time in weeks, I actually felt good. After the showdown with my parents over Preston, the showdown with *Preston* over Preston, and trying to get used to living in a sardine can, I wasn't in the best place in my life. Add to that feeling inadequate in my new position, and things weren't looking great for my mental health. My new boss's praise was exactly what I needed to thaw the chill that settled over me and feel alive again.

"I'm so glad you like it," I said.

Given more thought, I could have come up with something more eloquent or witty, but at that moment, that was all that seemed to matter. I was starting to reach for one of the sketches to ask how he felt about the color scheme and settle a debate I'd been having with myself when my stomach rumbled. It was loud enough to make my press my hand to it, and Nik laughed.

"Are you hungry?" he asked.

"Apparently so," I said. "I didn't stop for lunch today."

"Do you want to get something to eat?"

I shook my head. "No. That's all right. I don't need the break. I have a granola bar in my desk. I'll just eat that while I'm finishing some things up."

"I meant with me," he said, and my mouth went dry.

"With you?" I asked.

"Yeah. I barely ate any lunch either. Since we're both hungry, we should go grab some dinner," he suggested.

I opened my mouth to say something, then closed it and shook my head again.

"I really shouldn't. I should stay here and keep working. We don't have a lot of time left until the campaign starts, and I want to make sure everything's ready," I said.

Nik wasn't having it. He took the sketches from my hand and set them back down on the desk next to the copies he'd helped me make.

"As your boss and the one you are working so hard to impress by the campaign deadline, I'm pulling rank. You can't just keep driving yourself into the ground. We need to eat dinner. We might as well do it together so we can continue to talk marketing. We'll get plenty of work done, and it will help you get the rest of the project done even faster," he announced.

I laughed. "All right. You talked me into it. We'll grab something if you promise you'll tell me more about marketing and your strategy for the campaign."

"Are you negotiating with me?" he asked.

There was something warm in his voice, a hint of something more than a boss just casually asking to grab a bite to eat with his employee. I let a bit of a smile curve my lips.

"Maybe," I told him.

"All right. Something quick and then we'll come back to work," he said.

Turned out, Nik's idea of fast and simple was aligned right with my parents. And, let's be honest, me. Not that I never ate fast food and didn't appreciate the sheer joy of stuffing myself with greasy pizza or a doughnut bought at a drive-thru in the middle of the night when hanging out with Elly. But for the most part, eating meant dining, and that was something completely different. Which is why I immediately recognized the restaurant as Nik drove up to it in his sleek black car.

I'd been to the restaurant many times with my family

and friends. It was a very nice place and one where the customer service dictated everyone on staff would recognize me. The power of my father's name was wasted on very few people, especially those angling for his tips. It made me nervous as the valet opened the door and I stepped out to walk alongside Nik through the double doors. The host looked up from the podium and made eye contact with me but didn't go out of his way to acknowledge me. That very well could have meant the news of my self-excising from my family and striking out on my own preceded me, but it also could have meant the host was simply choosing to be discreet, as he was often called to do when people roamed through those doors with people hanging from their arms who shouldn't be there. Mistresses, cuckolds, inappropriately young flings, other peoples' wives and husbands, the children, and siblings of rivals. Enough scandal walked right into that restaurant. He didn't need to look anywhere else for it.

Whatever the reason he didn't call me by name or ask me how my family was, it was a relief. I hadn't told anyone at the company who I was or about my background. I'd even asked Elly and Devin not to tell anyone. I didn't want any of my new coworkers to know anything about my family or catch wind of the issues we were facing. For the first time in my life, I could really and fully decide who I wanted to be. And I just wanted to be a normal person, not a disinherited former heiress. If the staff acknowledged me, it would all be over. But none of them did. They simply whisked us to the most exclusive table in the restaurant, handed us menus, and backed away.

"This is beautiful," I told Nik.

"It's one of my favorite places," he said, looking around almost nostalgically.

Something about the look in his eyes emphasized his age, and I was surprised by the shiver of attraction that rippled through me. The waiter came up, and Nik ordered a bottle of wine. I recognized the name, and the year told me it was a very good, very expensive bottle. He said it completely nonchalantly, giving as much consideration to ordering it as anyone else would asking for a soda. When the waiter walked away, Nik turned his attention to me.

"So, Jane, what would you consider the ideal target demographic for the app?" he asked.

It felt almost like a trap, but at the same time, there wasn't any hint of testing in his voice. He really did bring me to get something to eat and talk about work. I took a sip of water to soothe the dryness of my mouth I seemed to not be able to get rid of since he'd found me in the copy room.

"Well, that's an interesting question. I know the idea of demographics and focusing efforts specifically toward those age ranges of people is a primary tenet of marketing. I just don't really buy into that. Not always, anyway," I told him.

The wine arrived and we paused as the sommelier presented the bottle to Nik, poured some into his glass, and awaited his approval before pouring more. The bottle set aside, the sommelier walked away from the table, and Nik held up his glass to me. He didn't make any specific toast, but we looked into each other's eyes for a beat. I tipped some of the garnet wine into my mouth, and immediately the rich flavor overtook my tongue. This was a strong, aggressive wine I wouldn't usually think of to drink before a meal. That said something impactful about Nik. This was a man who wasn't confined by convention or overly concerned with doing what was expected of him. He knew what he liked and didn't hesitate to have it.

"Is that what you think about the app?" he asked.

"Yes," I said. "I think something like an app is hard to bracket into one specific age range. Of course, there are exceptions, but users of technology range widely. Just like you talked about the sketches being fresh and classic, not alienating consumers. That's the way I feel about focusing too heavily on demographics. We don't want to zero in on one set of people when our most devoted users could be in the ones we're ignoring."

Nik grinned and took another sip of wine.

"Maybe I underestimated you, Jane."

I smiled back at him.

"I guess you shouldn't do that again," I teased.

"I guess I shouldn't. So, tell me about yourself." He tipped his head toward me like he wanted there to be a clear understanding. "Purely for research purposes, of course. So I don't underestimate you again."

"Of course. Um." My mind flipped through various details of my life, trying to settle on the ones I didn't mind revealing to him. "What do you want to know?"

"Where did you grow up?" Nik asked.

"New York born and bred," I told him. "I can't imagine it any other way."

"Neither can I. This is home. Few other places can even begin to compare," he said.

"How could they?" I asked. "It's the city that never sleeps."

"And that leaves so much time for so many other things."

I looked at him and couldn't help but notice the slight flash in his eyes. My last sip of wine warmed my belly, and I accepted a refill. In the moments of looking away from him, I managed to get my thoughts under control.

"Do you have any siblings?" I asked.

"No. I'm an only child," he answered.

"So am I," I told him, getting a strange amount of pleasure out of knowing we shared that experience. "My parents used to joke I was their 'cultivated child.' It would have been a lot cuter if it didn't actually feel like they were grooming me."

I said it before I even thought through the words, and as soon as I did, Nik's expression shift made me wish I hadn't.

"What do you mean?" he asked.

I took another long sip of wine to fill some of the silence and shook my head.

"Nothing. They were just very... adamant. They put a lot into making me into what they wanted me to be," I explained.

"That sounds familiar," he said. "Only my parents didn't even try to make it sound cute. If my father could have put me in a pot of soil, stuck me in the greenhouse, and pruned me until I was the exact specimen of a son he wanted, he would have."

I laughed. This dinner was definitely going differently than I imagined. After our feeble initial attempt, our conversation drifted away from work and into our lives, revealing we had a lot in common. And even more surprisingly, my new boss was actually funny. But it wasn't just his humor I was noticing. A warm feeling rolling through me could have been the wine, but it also could have been the way Nik was looking at me.

No. It was the wine. It had to be the wine. The last thing I needed to do was harbor a crush on my new boss. There were a lot of ways to fuck up my first ever job, but screwing my new boss would be a truly spectacular one. Only, he was proving himself to be infinitely screwable and increasingly difficult to resist. I told myself I had to resist temptation. I couldn't let myself keep toppling further into my attraction.

I took hold of my glass of wine and downed the rest of it to fortify myself.

Oh, shit. Wine is not what you want when you're trying to convince yourself not to crawl into someone's lap. I was tipsier than I thought. I looked across the table.

And Nik knew it.

CHAPTER 7

NIK

Jane took down a few glasses of wine between us sitting down at the table and finishing dinner, and I was starting to notice the effect it was having on her. She wasn't drunk. She still had her faculties about her and was carrying on a conversation with me, but there was definitely a change. Her eyes were decidedly slumbering, and her words slowed down. My protective instincts kicked in, and I felt the need to make sure she was all right. We were having a great time together, better even than I expected.

What started as just a fast dinner before we went back to work turned into more than two hours of sitting together talking, laughing, and working our way through several courses of decadent food. I loved the way she ate. There was no hesitation, none of that delicate, fragile poking at her plate and eating the garnishes rather than the food itself. I'd had those types of dates, and they never failed to completely turn me off. For Jane, eating was a sensual, sensory experience. She savored each bite, breathing in the aroma before sliding it off the utensil and into her mouth. The little sounds she made when she particularly liked something made my body ache. Her laugh only made it better.

But it still wasn't enough. I didn't want our time together to end. Even more important than that, I wanted to make sure she was all right. When she took the final lingering bite of her tiramisu, I smiled at her.

"Was it good?" I asked.

"Incredible," she answered.

"Good. I'm glad. I'm going to have my driver bring you home. I want to make sure you get there safe."

"I'm fine," she insisted. "It was just a couple of glasses."

"I'm sure you are," I said. "But humor me. I would feel much better knowing you got home all right. I'll make sure your car is brought to you, so you have it for tomorrow."

Jane nodded and I signaled for the waiter to bring the check. I did want to make sure she was getting home safe. A few glasses of wine might not leave someone stumbling around and not being able to make good choices, but it could make driving effectively a bit touch-and-go. But in the back of my mind, I was also thinking I could prolong my time with her just a little by accompanying her to her door. Even just a few more minutes sitting in the back seat with her would keep the rush of being close to her going. I usually drove myself to work and had driven to the restaurant, but as soon as I noticed the change in Jane, I sent a discreet text to my driver to have him come pick us up. I'd arrange for someone else to come pick up my other car and hers as well when she was safely home.

Once the check was paid, I tucked my card back in my billfold, slipped several bills into the check folder, and reached for Jane's hand. She let me help her up to her feet, and I guided her around in front of me. I put my hand in the small of her back and used it to gently escort her to the front of the restaurant. I could feel the warmth of her skin through the fabric of her shirt and wished there was nothing between my fingers and her body. She didn't pull away from my touch. As we got to the front door, she seemed to lean back into it, as if she thought any second, I'd stop touching her and she wanted to take in as much of it as she could.

I made a point not to move my hand away as we walked out of the restaurant and to the end of the walkway. My driver was already waiting there in my SUV, and I opened the back door for Jane. She slipped inside, and I climbed in after her. Her eyes slid to the side, and a slight smile curved her lips when I settled into the seat at her side.

"What's your address?" I asked.

She told me and I relayed it to my driver. He nodded in the rearview mirror and pulled away from the curb. I glanced over and saw Jane blushing fiercely as she looked down at her lap. When she noticed me watching her, she looked up and the color on her cheeks deepened.

"The vintage we were drinking must have been especially strong that year," she said.

I smiled. "It must have been."

Her tongue slid across her lips again, and her eyes flickered to my mouth. The heat was building between us, and right as it was getting to an intense, magnetic pressure that filled the entire cabin, she turned away to look out the window.

"I love that little bakery," she said, pointing to a shop as we drove by. "They make the best blueberry muffins. And croissants. Really good croissants."

"I'll have to try it sometime."

She nodded and pointed again. "That little boutique is where I got my prom dress. I barely remember my date, but the dress was amazing. And that pet shop is where my high school best friend had her first job. She was supposed to be an assistant groomer, but she dyed a poodle pink and got fired on her first weekend. Do you have any pets?"

The words came out of her in a stream with barely a breath or pause between the sentences.

"No," I told her. "I love dogs and have always wanted to have one, but I'm just not around the house enough. I wouldn't want to get a dog and then have it just sitting around alone all day because I'm too busy working."

"Maybe you could just not work so much," she said.

I gave a short laugh. "What a scandalous suggestion. How about you? Do you have a house full of pets?"

"No," she said, shaking her head.

"Because you work too much."

She shook her head again. "No."

I laughed. "Fair enough."

Jane searched the fronts of the shops, trying to come up with the next thing she was going to talk about. It was obvious she was just making nervous conversation, trying to cut the sexual tension between us. She pointed out the window again.

"See that cheese shop?"

She was adorable, but I couldn't take it anymore. I didn't want to hear her talk about any more of the shops. My finger held to her lips quieted her and Jane looked up at me. The hunger burning in them snapped my restraint, and I couldn't resist her for another minute. Pulling her close, I crushed my mouth over hers and kissed her passionately. There wasn't any hesitation from Jane. She didn't seem demure or try to pull back. She responded with as much intensity and passion as I had, her hands sliding up my chest so her arms could wrap around my neck. Our kiss deepened and I wrapped an arm around her waist to pull her up into my lap.

As our mouths tangled and played across each other, I let my hands explore the curves and dips of her body. My fingers eagerly pulled on the crisp white blouse tucked into her black skirt. It released, letting my hand tuck under the fabric and onto the smooth skin of her back. The way she sat made the small of her back arch, and I let my fingers trace the graceful curve. I couldn't stop kissing her, couldn't stop touching her. I didn't realize how long we'd been engrossed with each other until the SUV stopped. I pulled myself reluctantly away from her and we both peered out the window.

"That's my building," she said in a breathy tone.

She slid off my lap and adjusted her skirt as I got out of the car. Reaching in for her, I took her hand and helped her out.

"I'll walk you to your door," I said.

Jane nodded and we made our way into the building. It was dimly lit and felt close, almost suffocating, but I followed her up the flight of stairs and onto the next. By the middle of the second flight, I was starting to feel reservations. As we climbed the third flight, alarm bells were going off in my head. The overprotective part of my mind wanted to scoop Jane up and take her far away from the unpleasant building.

That compulsion didn't lessen when we got to her apartment door. She unlocked it and stepped inside, turning back to me.

"Thank you for walking me to my door," she said. "Would you like to come inside?"

I wouldn't have gone so far as to say I wanted to go in, but curiosity and the desire to be near Jane beat out the uncertainty the building made me feel, and I went inside. Looking around at the space, I frowned. It was tiny and spilling over with belongings that didn't seem to fit, both in terms of space and their style. Much of what had been wedged into the minuscule apartment was paintings and art supplies. It was too small and cramped for someone like Jane, but she moved through it without hesitation, heading into the kitchen. She didn't seem completely comfortable, as if it wasn't quite like home. She came back a few seconds later with a bottle of wine and two glasses.

"Would you like a glass of wine?" she asked.

I scoffed and reached for the bottle. "I think you've had enough wine." I took one of the glasses and carried both back into the kitchen, where I filled it with water and handed it to her. "Drink this instead."

She took the glass and downed a sip. I looked at her expectantly, and she glared back.

"You know, I'm not on the clock now. I don't have to take orders from you," she said.

I wanted to laugh, but I stopped myself and maintained my stern expression until she relented and finished off the rest of the water. She leaned around me to set the glass on the counter. We were standing close enough for me to breathe in her enchanting scent. It made me almost dizzy with my need for her. I knew I should go. This wasn't where I should be, and these definitely weren't the thoughts I should be having, but I couldn't. I couldn't drag myself away from her and walk out of the apartment without touching her again.

I leaned in closer, and Jane brushed her face against mine. Our mouths swept over each other, and finally we were kissing again. I yanked her up against me and kissed her harder, holding tight to her hips. My tongue plunged into her mouth, and she let out a whimpering moan. That was enough to push me over the edge. If I would have been able to resist her or try to walk away before, there was no way I could have now.

Picking her up, I set her down on the edge of the kitchen counter and pushed her knees apart so I could step between her thighs. She pressed forward against me as I eased her skirt up higher. My fingers made quick work of the buttons down the front of her shirt, and I pushed it away to reveal her lacy white bra. Cupping her breasts in my hands, I kneaded them and dipped my head to run my tongue through the valley between them.

Jane took hold of my shoulders and sighed, arching toward me and letting her head fall back. I kissed my way across one breast and peeled down the lace to take her nipple into my mouth. There was no turning back. Nothing was enough for me. I had to have her. All of her. As Jane pulled her arms from the sleeves of her shirt, I reached behind her to release the clasp of her bra. It popped open and the lace fell away from her full breasts.

In one movement, I gathered her against me, and Jane wrapped her legs around my waist. Her high heels fell to the kitchen floor as I carried her out and toward the hall I noticed while standing in the living room. The tiny space did have one benefit. It made it very easy to find her bedroom.

CHAPTER 8

JANE

This was not in my life plan. When I told my parents they weren't going to marry me off and walked away with the intention of building a life for myself, I made the vow I was going to stand on my own two feet. Which I was definitely not doing at the moment. In fact, my two feet were wrapped around my boss, along with every other part of me.

And I wasn't about to stop it.

Nik carried me down the hall into my bedroom. I might have wondered how he knew how to get there if I wasn't fully aware my entire apartment could probably nestle comfortably in his living room. Possibly even his bathroom. I squealed as he pulled me away from his body and tossed me onto my bed. I bounced on the mattress, then moved up toward the head of the bed, pushing aside my throw pillows. Nik stood at the foot of the bed, staring at me with hunger in his eyes. There wasn't even the slightest hint of hesitation around him. His desire was obvious, and I felt caught in the power of his energy. Not that I was complaining.

His eyes didn't move away from me as he unbuttoned his shirt and let it fall to the floor. As he took his shoes off, I wriggled out of my skirt and hose. Down to only the slim-fitting trunks that showed off a chiseled body and growing bulge, Nik climbed onto the bed with me. I crawled toward him, and we met in the middle of the bed on our knees. Our bodies touched, the heat of our skin searing against each other. My fingers dug into Nik's thick blond hair, and he ran his hands down my sides, so they grazed my ribs and settled into my waist before he grabbed my ass. One hard yank pulled me up against him, so the bulge of his hardening erection pressed into my belly. It made my mouth water with the promise of what was to come and my body ache for more.

My thighs slid farther apart, and Nik dipped his hand into my panties, his fingers slipping between my legs to brush against my core. I was already wet, but his touch sent a surge of heat that made me hold on to his hair tighter and gasp against his mouth. He swept his fingers through my folds another time, then withdrew his hand so he could guide my panties down my hips. I adjusted my legs so he could pull them off, leaving me fully bare and open in his hands. We kissed more intensely, and he tipped me backward, so I landed on the bed with my head on the pillows. I laughed as he lunged forward to bury his head in the curve of my neck and shoulder and pressed a row of kisses down to my collarbone. Nik's hand filling with my breast and his palm brushing against the taut peak of my nipple turned the sound into a gasp, and my eyes closed.

Nik kissed down to my breast and ran his tongue around my other nipple until it strained and ached. After a few seconds, I pulled him up, so he looked down into my face.

"Things seem a little one-sided here," I said through my panting breaths and tugged on the waistband of his boxers.

He shook his head. "Not yet."

His head dipped down again and started a new trail of kisses down the center of my chest onto my stomach. My muscles shook as he blew a cool stream of air onto my dampened skin. His hands pushed my thighs apart and held them down. I was completely exposed, totally at Nik's mercy. I should have felt vulnerable, but I didn't. Being in his hands made me feel beautiful and desired, and every inch of me craved more. He awakened something inside me, and I couldn't wait to explore more.

Nik nibbled his way down my stomach, and I bit down on my bottom lip to hold back a cry when his tongue finally swept through my folds the way his fingers had. The tip found the hypersensitive peak of my clit and flicked across it. I arched and he closed his mouth down over me, simultaneously sucking and continuing to swirl with his tongue. It was masterful, and I was rapidly losing myself in the intensity of the sensation. Knowing he was bringing me close to the brink and not wanting it to be over so fast, I pulled him up again. Kissing him did nothing to slow the racing of my heart and the arousal coursing through me, but it gave my body a chance to calm down slightly. Again, I reached for his trunks, and this time he let me push them off.

As soon as Nik kicked away the boxers, I pushed on his chest to flip him onto his back. I brought my mouth to his ear, close enough to brush it with my lips as I whispered to him.

"My turn."

Replicating the pattern of his kisses on my eager body, I ran my lips along his skin from the soft dip just beneath his ear along the side of his neck and onto his chest. They followed the rippling of his abs down and found the trail of hair leading from his navel. I happily hopped on and let it bring me down to exactly where I wanted to be. I hadn't let myself look when he first took off his boxers, so now I was getting the full experience. His cock was long and thick, everything I wanted as I wrapped my hand around the base. I ran my hand along it, but it wasn't enough for Nik. He wrapped his hand around mine, tightening my grip and guiding my strokes. His hiss of pleasure spurred me forward and I continued the rhythm he set for me.

When I couldn't take the craving anymore, I opened my mouth and drew my tongue over the head in a long lick. Relishing the taste of him, I delved further, tracing the slit with the tip of my tongue before opening my mouth and taking him in fully. I brought him as far as I could until the engorged head of his cock rested near my throat and my lips wrapped around the base. Moving my hands to his thighs so I could take in more, I rolled my tongue around his shaft.

Nik's hand cupped the back of my head, and he groaned as my mouth slid up and down over him. The head dipped into my throat, and I hummed my pleasure of feeling every inch of him. My eyes closed and I savored the smoothness of his skin and the swell of his veins.

It was only a few moments before he took hold of my shoulders and pulled me up, forcing me to release him. His strong grip guided me up to his body, so I straddled his hips. He held his cock in one hand and wrapped the other arm around my hips to pull me down onto him. My head fell back, and a gasp of sheer pleasure poured from my throat as I sank down to settle onto him. He filled me until I felt my body stretching to accommodate him. Nik sat up, pressing one hand onto the bed behind him for leverage as the other tightened around my hips.

I couldn't hold back my gasps and cries as he thrust up into me. He was relentless and commanding, but the touch of his mouth on my neck was reassuring and tender. I adjusted my legs so they wrapped around him again, and Nik changed his movements so his hips rocked against mine. It drove him deep into me, every thrust helping my body soften and open up more to hold him. I let my hips relax, trying to open them up to bring more of him in.

Nik kissed me hard and I held on tightly to him, my arms wrapped around his shoulders so my breasts crushed against his chest. In one sudden movement, he flipped me onto my back again. He stayed buried inside me and propped himself up with his hands on either side of my shoulders to thrust faster and deeper. A fine sheen of sweat formed on his skin, and I rose up to lick some from his chest. I couldn't believe how much fun I was having and the amount of pleasure I was getting from him.

From my boss.

It shouldn't have been that incredible. He was at least fifteen years older than me and the insanely powerful head of the company where I had my first job. It should have felt wrong, but somehow that only made it hotter.

I grabbed his hips and pulled him in deeper, encouraging him to sink harder into me. One arm swept under my leg to prop it on his shoulder, creating a new angle that was almost unbearably incredible. He caught my deep groan with his mouth and went into an almost frenzied pace. I dug my fingernails into his back and met each of his thrusts with a lift of my hips, grinding my body against his. Our skin slipped and slid across each other with our sweat, and I could barely breathe the pleasure became so intense.

All at once, my orgasm hit me. The sensations reached a peak that held Nik tight and pulled him in deep. Every inch of my body lit up, and my mind went blank. I screamed into his mouth, the sound blending with his guttural groan as his cock gave a hard pulse and he tumbled into his own climax.

Nik collapsed down on top of me, his kiss turning soft and languid. Our lips brushed and our tongues lightly swept across each other until my warm, satisfied body sank down into the mattress and my eyes drifted closed. Totally satiated by the remarkable night of passion, I fell asleep thinking my boss wasn't the man I thought he was. It turned out he was pretty amazing.

It also turned out he was quiet as all hell because when I woke up the next morning, Nik was gone. In his place was a raging hangover. I didn't think I'd had that much to drink the night before, but not drinking enough water combined with the settling realization I'd just fucked my new boss was contributing to the matter. This was so many levels of inappropriate. It had seemed like a fantastic idea when we were in the back seat of the SUV, where he was running his hands all over me. Now in the light of day, as much as I could get in the dark little shoebox that was my new apartment, it didn't seem like such a great plan. Nik's clandestine disappearance at some point in the night wasn't helping matters. I was worried about what he was thinking and what might happen next. There was only one thing to do.

"I fucked him," I said flatly.

"We have seriously got to work on your phone greeting etiquette," Elly said.

"I'm sorry. Hi, Elly."

"Hi, Jane. Who are we talking about?"

"Nik Nygard," I said.

She made a gagging sound, and I could only imagine she was choking on her morning orange juice. I probably should have made sure she wasn't consuming anything before I dropped the hammer on her. That could be potentially hazardous.

"Nik Nygard, as in mega-powerful CEO Nik Nygard?" she asked.

"Yes. Nik Nygard, as in my new boss Nik Nygard." I groaned and covered my eyes with my hand. "I can't believe I did that. When I thought about climbing the corporate ladder, climbing my boss wasn't exactly what I had in mind."

"How did it happen?" she asked.

I gave her a brief rundown of the night before.

"And now he's not here and I'm possibly standing at the threshold of my own personal hell," I told her.

"That was a seriously rookie mistake when starting a new job, but I can't really blame you since I sort of did something similar with my own husband," Elly pointed out.

I glared at the phone even though I knew she couldn't see me.

"Yeah, I don't think that really applies here. I am not seeing us ending up married. It was probably just a one-night thing, over and forgotten," I said.

Elly laughed. "Maybe that's what you should do. Just forget it happened."

"That's a good idea," I told her.

"It wasn't an idea. It was a joke. You can't actually forget that," she pointed out.

I ignored her. My strategy was already in place. I was just going to go about my life, pretending nothing happened.

CHAPTER 9

NIK

I'd never been one to try to avoid conflict. There were people who couldn't stand the idea and get away as fast as they can, avoiding it at all costs. Not me. I always headed into it full-on, ready to settle it. Of course, there had rarely been a time in my life when I wasn't the dominant force in any confrontation, so dealing with conflict wasn't really an issue.

Until I got into a conflict with myself. Then it wasn't so easy. That's what I was dealing with the next morning when I was getting ready for work. Rolling out of bed and calling my driver to pick me up in the middle of the night wasn't exactly the best form. I wanted it to seem like I was giving Jane space to think everything through for herself and decide how she felt about what had happened. Or at the very least save her the uncomfortable rituals of the morning after two people who were just starting to know each other had sex. Those awkward moments when they skated around each other, trying to figure out getting dressed, showering, eating breakfast... all those things that seem totally mundane until you're trying to do them along-side someone you're not in a relationship with but have just tumbled around naked with.

What it actually made me look like was a heartless jackass who got what I wanted and dipped as soon as the opportunity arose.

I should have stayed. I wanted to stay. When Jane fell asleep in my arms, it felt so perfect. I wanted to watch her sleep until I fell asleep and spent the night right there beside her. But then, there it was. The conflict.

Being with Jane was amazing. I wanted to do it again as soon as possible, but there were still a few issues we needed to work out. She'd had a few glasses of wine, but she wasn't drunk, so consent wasn't the problem. However, it was very possible she was feeling a little friendlier after most of the bottle went into her. The more glaring issue was that I was her boss. My position of power over her put us in a gray area. I was going to have to tread carefully. I didn't want to give her the impression I was taking advantage of her or trying to use her. And I didn't want anyone else in the office thinking she was getting perks by fucking the boss. That wasn't even close to what this was. At least, not to me. I didn't see the night before as a chance thing or Jane as a one-night stand. I knew there was more to it. I'd known it the moment I'd first laid eyes on her.

That is, if she wanted there to be. I wasn't technically her direct supervisor, so HR wouldn't have a field day about us. There were ways to negotiate an office relationship that wouldn't compromise the integrity of the company or the rest of the team.

I couldn't believe I was actually considering a relation-ship with Jane. I hadn't even really dated since my divorce ten years before. A few scattered dinners, escorting women to gala events, and one-off flings here and there didn't exactly count as forming close bonds. Not that my marriage had been that much of a fairy tale either. In fact, it wasn't really much of a relationship at all. I was always busy trying to build up my business and hadn't had much time for Angela. After the very brief honeymoon period wore off, we'd barely spent any real time together. There were no romantic evenings spent cuddling in front of the fireplace or long, leisurely vacations taken just for the purpose of enjoying each other. It didn't excuse her from cheating on me, but I could understand why she did. She'd needed a level of attention and love I wasn't giving her.

I might not have been capable of giving it to her. I was far too focused on myself and my professional aspirations to put any energy or attention on nurturing my relationship with her. I wouldn't admit it then, but I absolutely took Angela for granted. I figured she would always be there. We were married, so that was it. She was my wife, and our marriage was what it was. It was a cold dose of reality when I had to face not just the realization that my marriage had failed, but also that I'd pushed her away.

I wasn't still clinging to Angela. Any feelings I'd had for her in that way had dissipated many years before, but the lessons I learned from that marriage still hung on strong. I knew there wasn't any point in getting into another relationship if the same thing would happen again. I didn't want to put myself into the position of having another woman putting her love and devotion into me if I wasn't able to give it to her in return. It was more than that. It was more than just a sense of responsibility and duty. It was wanting more for Jane. I wouldn't want to neglect her or make her feel like she wasn't special, but by the way I was feeling already, I didn't think that was too likely. She was all I could think about.

I knew I needed to talk to Jane about what had happened. We needed to clear the air and figure out exactly where we stood. That morning I had a meeting with the marketing team, and as I went into the office, I saw the perfect opportunity to talk to her. As I walked down the hallway, I caught her alone in the conference room. She was walking around the table, setting information packets at each place. I wanted to just stand there and watch her. The way she moved was so graceful and elegant. Without even trying, she was captivating. As she leaned forward to position another package in front of a chair diagonal from her, her hair slipped over her back and down her shoulder so it hung in a curtain over her face. I had the compulsion to go into the room and sweep it out of the way, but I knew if I touched the silky strands or breathed in her warm, sweet smell, I wouldn't be able to stop myself.

I would need to have her right then, right there. That was definitely not something I could risk. Negotiating an office romance was one thing. Taking her on the conference room table ten minutes before a meeting with the entire department was something completely different. But that didn't stop me from fantasizing about it.

She looked up at me as she moved around to the opposite side of the table and caught sight of me standing at the door.

"Good morning, Mr. Nygard," she said.

That should have sounded cold and dismissive, not so sexy it chipped away at my resolve. I took a step closer to the table.

"Good morning, Jane," I said. "I think we've gotten to the place where you can call me Nik."

She flashed me a tight smile, but didn't respond. After setting down the last of the packets, she glanced up at me.

"Everything is ready here. The meeting isn't for another couple of minutes, so I'm going to go to the break room and get a cup of coffee and a muffin. Can I bring you back anything?"

She started to move around me, but I stepped into her path to block her way to the door. I didn't want her running away from me right then. We needed to talk about this, and if she got out of the room, the others would be here before she got back. I'd have to wait, and I didn't think I could make it through the meeting without her saying something about what happened between us.

"Jane, just wait a second. I want to talk to you about last night," I started.

She shook her head almost frantically, as if she thought she could stop the words from getting into her ears.

"No," she said, sounding flustered. "We really don't need to do that."

"But, Jane," I tried again, but she looked directly into my eyes.

"Really. No discussion is necessary. In fact, it's probably best if we don't talk about it again. It was an impulsive decision, and it's behind us now. Let's not make it weird by having some big talk about it. Just pretend it didn't happen that's what I'm planning on doing," she said.

I started to disagree, but voices coming down the hallway stopped me. A second later, Maddie, Ethan, and Toby came into the room. They stopped when they entered, and Ethan looked back and forth between Jane and me.

"Is everything all right?" he asked.

They seemed to be able to feel the tension between us, but I wasn't going to acknowledge it. Not to them. If Jane wasn't ready to talk about what happened between us, there was no way I was going to open it up for a roundtable discussion with the rest of the marketing team.

"Of course," I said. "Jane was just saying she was going to the break room for coffee and a muffin, and I was saying a muffin sounded great."

She nodded and walked around me, easing through the small group gathered just inside the door to head to the break room. I smiled and gestured at the table for the others to take their places. They sat down and started flipping through the packets Jane left on the table. She came back a few moments later and handed me a muffin wrapped in a napkin before sitting in the chair farthest from me.

"All right let's get started," I said. "If everyone will open up your packets, we can discuss the direction we're going with the campaign and the next steps we're going to take."

Jane's sketches looked incredible and seeing them pieced together with the verbiage for the print, TV, and social ads made them even better. The campaign was coming alive, and it was exciting, but we weren't completely there, yet. We had sketches and words, but we needed more.

"Have we decided where we're going to shoot the campaign?" Toby asked a few minutes later after we'd gone over the approach.

"Where we shoot the ad images is going to be critical. We need something dynamic that will stand out to consumers. Something identifiable but not gimmicky. We want to appeal to them and take advantage of emotions and thoughts already established by the imagery, but don't want to seem pandering or derivative," I said.

Everyone bandied around ideas for a few seconds, but nothing felt exactly right. A few of the ideas stood out as unique, but I worried we wouldn't be able to match them seamlessly with the rest of the campaign. Others were too mundane and would look washed-out against the bold energy we were trying to achieve.

"How about Paris?" Jane asked.

All the attention of the table turned to her.

"Paris?" Ethan asked.

She looked up from the papers in front of her, glancing around almost as if she was surprised anyone had even heard her suggestion much less was willing to listen to it.

"Well... yes. It's classic and familiar, but that's not necessarily a bad thing. It has the sophistication we were going for in the campaign, and if we use the right locations and approach to the images, it can have the edge. That in of itself will communicate the type of message we want. A company that is solid, dependable, stylish, elegant, roman-tic, sophisticated, maybe a little sexy... just like the city, but at the same time, with an unexpected slant, an edge that highlights a new perception of what is established, a new way to see what they already know and think. It demon-strates reliability and security, but control and readiness to move with the times and take the world by storm," Jane explained.

The explanation was almost breathtaking. It was exactly what I wanted. Without waiting for anyone else to respond, I nodded.

"Yes," I said.

"It's perfect," Maddie agreed.

"So, it's settled. The team will fly to Paris for a week for the shoots," I announced.

Toby gave an excited nod. "I'll get the arrangements in place."

"The team?" Jane asked, sounding surprised.

"Yes," I said. "The team. "We all need to be there to make sure we achieve the right vibe. Everyone's input will be important."

It was true, but that didn't change the thoughts now running through my head. I wondered what it would be like to spend a week in Paris with Jane. Maybe I would get another chance to talk about what happened between us. And what might happen next.

CHAPTER 10

JANE

I couldn't believe what I'd just heard. Nik said the team. The whole marketing team. And as a member of the marketing team, that meant me. I got to go along on the trip for the shoot. I was beyond excited at the prospect of traveling to Paris. Even if it was a business trip and not a vacation for relaxation or pleasure, it was *Paris*. It didn't matter the circumstances, there was never a time when I wouldn't look forward to visiting Paris. It was my favorite city, beautiful, romantic, and inspirational. I used to spend every spring there, before the unfortunate incident with my parents that led to me being cut off. Without access to the seemingly endless family funds, I had no way of just hopping a jet and spending weeks lazily strolling the streets and painting.

As much as the idea of going back to the beloved city thrilled me, I couldn't help but think about how this trip was actually going to go. I wasn't just going on a business trip to Paris. I was going to be working in Paris with my handsome, sexy boss who I'd slept with. that put a whole new spin on it. The romance of the city, the dreaminess of being away from the reality of my current circumstances, my longing to repeat what happened... all that was going to make things tough. The more the team talked about the trip and started putting plans into place for the locations of the shoot, the more I envisioned being there. I knew the city so well and could easily bring to mind images of the places they mentioned. Some of the things they said made me wonder if Maddie or Ethan had ever traveled to Paris. They didn't talk about it with the type of familiarity and fondness of someone who'd walked those streets and peered through the windows of the tiny shops or sat at the cafés and just watched life bloom around them.

The more I listened, the more I told myself it would be fine. It had to be. I would just keep on with the plan of pretending the night before didn't happen. It wouldn't be easy. It especially wouldn't be easy being around Nik in the City of Lights, but I didn't have a choice. I was going to prove to myself and to everyone else I could be professional and handle the job. Even if that meant swallowing all my feelings and forcing myself to go on like nothing had changed. Being in Paris was going to be a trial by fire. Getting through that without letting my feelings, or my body, take over would prove to me, and to Nik, I would be able to carry on into the future as long as I held on to the job.

The conversation shifted away from where we would stage the shoots and to the arrangements that needed to be made. Toby could handle booking the flights, but a debate rose up about where to reserve our accommodations. Maddie was usually the one to make those types of arrangements. I'd learned that a few days after I started working there when I heard her complaining that Ethan had asked her to book him a flight and hotel for a shoot in Florida.

Listening to her bemoan the difference between an assistant director and assistant *to* the director was hilarious, though I wasn't comfortable enough with her at the time to tell her. Getting a room in a hotel in Florida was easy, but that didn't quite translate over to Paris. Having never been, just as I suspected, she didn't know where to look for the right spot.

"We need to find something that's easy for all of us to stay close together, and where our equipment will be safe," Ethan said.

Nik's eyes slid over to him, but he didn't say anything.

"I think we can manage to find somewhere with a low crime rate in Paris," he said.

I held back my laugh by staring down at the papers on the table in front of me. When the meeting ended, I hung back to talk to Maddie. When the others left, I walked up to the assistant director, who turned to me with a bright smile.

"Are you excited?" she asked. "Your first business trip!"

"Yeah. It should be a good time," I told her. "Actually, I might be able to help you with the arrangements, too."

"Oh?" she asked, stuffing the rest of her stuff into her satchel and picking it up from the table.

"I know a rental place in Paris that could be perfect. It has a great studio space and several bedrooms," I said.

"How do you know it?" Maddie asked.

"I took some art classes in Paris when I was younger and I stayed there," I answered.

I purposely avoided telling her I'd actually rented the place myself, so I had a more comfortable home base during my time in Paris. I figured telling her that would earn me some strange looks and a few questions I didn't want to answer.

"That actually sounds great. Send me the information and I'll look into it. Having something like that sounds better for collaboration than us all staying in different hotel rooms," Maddie said.

"Absolutely. We'd all have our own space in the separate bedrooms, but then could easily get together in the common areas and keep the equipment and work in the same place so it's accessible," I told her.

"That would be perfect. Thanks for your help."

I smiled, happy to feel helpful. I still felt like I was earning my place on the team. None of the others were making me feel that way. They were all welcoming and encouraging, but I still had the sense I was a little bit outside a bubble they were in. Having my suggestion chosen for the location of the shoot and now being able to guide Maddie to the rental made me feel like I was getting closer to really being a part of it all.

After swinging by the break room for another cup of coffee and my second muffin of the day, I went back to my office. There were still a few things I wanted to work on and adjustments I wanted to make to the sketches. Now that I knew we were shooting the ads in Paris, I wanted to get started on a few more options so there would be plenty to choose from. I knew the photographer and Ethan would have plenty of visions for the pictures they were taking, but that didn't stop my mind from overflowing with ideas. I wanted to sketch out a few of the visions I had so I could suggest them before the trip.

But sliding peacefully back into work and dreaming of Paris was not to be. I left my phone on my desk during the meeting, and when I got there, I noticed I had a message. Nibbling on the muffin and poking through to find the best blueberries inside, I listened to the voicemail.

"Jane, this is your mother. Your father and I have not heard from you and can only take that as you are digging in your heels. You are trying to prove your point and waiting for us to come to you. Well, here I am. You can stop this now. Stop being ridiculous. Everyone knows you are not cut out for the life you've put yourself in. You were bred for much more than that. You were not made to live on your own in the dregs of town, barely scraping by and having no social life to speak of. Think of this realistically, Jane. Do you really want to stay in that cramped, dismal apartment for the rest of your life when you could be living in the Howell mansion?"

The message ended and I sighed, but that wasn't it. There was another message, and I could only imagine who it was from. But as much as I wanted to, I couldn't ignore it. She would just keep calling, and I didn't want to deal with that either.

"Jane, please. Be reasonable. I understand you are trying to assert yourself and take on the world, but you need to understand that your father and I know what's best for you. We only want to make sure you have the very best life possible. Ever since you were born, we dreamed of what your future would be and the kind of life you would have. When you were a little girl, you loved to throw little tea parties for your dolls and stuffed animals, and then galas for your Barbies. You were always looking forward to the next event or party, and you always made friends so easily. You were made for society, Jane. Right now, you are toiling away at some job and probably barely making ends meet. And for what? Just to say that's what you're doing? So, you can attend the building block party? Or eat grocery store cake when it's the birthday of someone in the office? That's not you. Wouldn't you much rather be the wife of a wealthy man who will ensure you never want for anything? Who can provide whatever you want? Wouldn't you rather be hosting the best parties and surrounding yourself with the best people? Think about it. I know you know the truth."

That message warranted an even bigger sigh. I'd forgotten how much my mother looked down on people without money. I didn't even think she realized it. It's not that she thought they were inherently bad or hated them. She interacted with them just fine when she had the opportunity to. Yet, there was a deep-seated sense of privilege and social hierarchy that fueled her along, and there was nothing changing it. Being away from it only highlighted the stark trait for me. I wanted to dive into my work, but still couldn't. There was yet one more message, and I had to get through that one, too. I started it with high hopes it would be brief.

"Jane, it's time to come to your senses and recognize the reality of the situation. You are not where you belong, and you are putting yourself through this for truly absurd reasons. Never in your life did you shy away from luxury or the privileges given to you. You always knew how to make the very most out of the life afforded to you by your father and me. Now you are being nothing but selfish. We have done everything since the day you were born to make sure you had every opportunity, every privilege. You went to the best schools, were given the best art lessons and tutors. Your debut is still talked about as the most spectacular any of our friends ever attended. We have done everything to ensure your life would be everything it could, and all we ask in return is for you to trust us. This marriage is not only in your best interest, but it is also in the best interest of the family and the Howells. Your stubbornness affects people, you know. It isn't just you. We are willing to put this whole nasty mess aside and completely absolve you if you make the right decision. Your trust fund is still waiting for you, and your father has already contacted the very best designers and planners to create the wedding of your dreams. It's time to start your real life again, Jane."

The monotone voice telling me there were no more messages was a glorious sound. My mother was right in some of what she said. I always did fully immerse myself in the luxury offered to me. It was what I knew, and I didn't have much of a concept of anything else. But I didn't want that life anymore. Not if it came with my parents' constant control. I was much better off on my own, even if my apartment was cramped and just a touch dismal.

Besides, soon I would be in Paris.

CHAPTER 11

NIK

Brochures of Paris like to talk up things like the Eiffel Tower and the Louvre. Travel agents wax poetic about the quaint villages and the sweet little bakeries and cafés tucked away in corners just waiting to be discovered. If people were to believe what they saw on advertisements for vacations there, they'd think everyone walks in slow motion and is instantly beautiful when they arrive. They never said shit about the tiny little cobblestone streets that weave around aimlessly and are impossible to drag a suitcase over.

Of course, this was the first time I'd ever rolled my suitcase over much of anything, much less a cobbly-ass street barely bigger than a sidewalk. When I traveled, I was accustomed to a higher level of service. People opened doors for me. My luggage simply showed up in my hotel room after I checked in. Very often a butler unpacked it for me, and I didn't have to look at the suitcases again until it was time to leave.

Not this time. All that got left out of this particular trip to Paris. I was rolling one suitcase and carrying another under my arm, while carrying a third in the other hand as Toby hobbled along beside me, equally weighed down. We'd been going on this way for the last twenty minutes. Ahead of us, Jane led Maddie off the main road and into a small alley. Perfect. That was exactly what we needed. Getting lost and ending up targeted as the most touristy of tourists ripe for the picking. Today was not a day I felt like having to pummel someone for threatening Jane.

Ethan wasn't with us. A last-minute emergency meant he was going to have to take a different flight and would be meeting up with us tomorrow. As Toby and I made it to the alley and followed the women, I wondered if somehow the marketing director knew this was going to happen and had made a choice to skip out on it.

"Any idea how much longer?" I called up to the women.

They were chatting between themselves and searching the buildings. Maddie tossed a look back over her shoulder.

"Jane says the entrance is right along here somewhere. She knows where she is, we're just looking for it," she called to us.

It didn't give me a lot of encouragement when they continued right on down the alley and out onto another of the tiny streets. These cobblestone paths were far too narrow for a cab, hence the luggage train. We'd had to give up on driving almost as soon as we entered the city, and I was rapidly losing hope we were going to get anywhere. The women each had their carry-on bags and a rolling suit-case, but that left Toby and me with everything else. This included not just our personal luggage, but also bags of the equipment we weren't leaving to the photographer. Storyboards, Jane's sketches, vision boards, and wardrobe-filled bags Toby and I lugged along. It seemed like a good idea to keep those things with us rather than shipping them ahead.We thought it would take away the stress of worrying the items would get lost or not arrive on time or get damaged. Now I was strongly contemplating just leaving it and coming back for it when I found some sort of vehicle that would make it down the street.

And all this because Jane had insisted she knew the perfect place for us to stay in Paris. Maddie made the announcement with great flourish when we had our last meeting before the trip. Our flights were booked, the photographer was ready, model selection was underway. All that was left was finding out what hotel Maddie had reserved for us so we could be ready to travel. Turned out, it was no hotel. She'd skipped the conventional wisdom of securing rooms in a comfortable, reputable hotel where we could order room service and have our clothes dry-cleaned, and instead had rented an apartment Jane told her about.

This didn't fill me with excitement and confidence. I was familiar with what Jane considered an apartment. I'd seen where she lived and was several degrees separated from impressed. Finally, the women stopped ahead of us, and Jane looked back.

"Here it is," she announced.

Toby and I caught up with them and found they were standing in front of a plain, nondescript door. No plaque. No name. Nothing to differentiate it from every other door we'd walked past. I wondered how Jane had even found out about such a hole-in-the-wall place like this. She seemed to be excited she'd found it, but I was holding back any sense of relief until I actually got inside. I still wasn't convinced this was going to be an acceptable place for us to stay. If we got inside and it was anything like Jane's apartment back in New York, I was walking out without putting the luggage down. We'd call around until we found a decent hotel and figure out how to cancel the rental of the apartment later.

Jane took a deep breath and turned the knob to throw the door open. I was instantly surprised by what I saw. The door opened into a lovely entryway, clean, airy, and elegantly decorated. She stepped inside and gestured for us to follow her, sweeping her hand through the space like she was presenting it. As soon as I stepped inside, I knew I had to start trusting Jane's instincts.

She led us farther into the building and up a short flight of steps to another door. Maddie reached into her pocket and withdrew her phone. She scrolled through a few screens, then held it up as she input a code into the electronic keypad beside the door. A lock clicked and Jane opened the door to lead us the rest of the way inside. She seemed comfortable in the space, as if she knew it well. It was unexpected, and I made a mental note to find out more about it.

I had to admit the apartment was impressive. All my concerns and hesitation disappeared when I stepped inside and let myself admire the surroundings. Sprawling common rooms gave us plenty of places to spread everything out and work together, and a long hallway led to another wing where I assumed the bedrooms were located. I couldn't help but continue to wonder how Jane had somewhere like this tucked in her back pocket. It wasn't a place a casual visitor to the city would just happen upon. And I sincerely doubted it was listed on any sort of vacation rental site.

It was clearly expensive. Very expensive. And it didn't

take much examination of the space to know the company's investment into renting it would be worth it.

"Can you believe this light?" Maddie crowed, standing in the center of the living room and spinning around with her arms spread out to her sides.

Tall windows taking up most of the wall spilled bright sunlight across the floor and brightened even the far corners of the room.

"It's perfect," Jane agreed. "And there are three other rooms on this side that have fantastic light, too. You can throw open the curtains and it's just incredible. We could even shoot some things here in the apartment."

"We could," Maddie agreed. "And along the street, too. That gives us even more options. We could take a huge number of pictures, everything we can come up with, and then go through them when we get back to the office so we can find the exact right ones."

"The kitchen is gorgeous. Do any of us know how to cook?" Jane asked. Maddie laughed and Jane gestured for her to follow her. "The common rooms are great but wait until you see the bedrooms. Grab your bags. If we hurry, we can claim the ones we want before the men get ahold of them."

Maddie giggled again and followed her into the depths of the apartment. When it was quiet again, I took a minute to look around and really take in the space. The architecture of the apartment created an open, airy feeling that flowed from one room to the other. Flawless high-polish wood floors accentuated elegant white furniture. A cornflower-blue blanket draped over one corner of the couch and matching plush pillows tucked into the corners invited visitors to lounge and read one of the countless volumes lining a wide bookshelf that stretched from the floor up to the crown molding. A narrow ladder on wheels designed to glide along the shelf rested against the sidewall.

Leaving my luggage where it was, I made my way farther into the apartment. Eventually I found my way to the kitchen Jane mentioned. It was definitely not the postage-stamp-sized kitchen of most apartments. This was the stuff of gourmet magazines and foodie daydreams. A copper hood shone over a double oven, and the island in the center was almost the size of some kitchen tables I'd seen. Granite countertops had me imagining what Jane would look like propped up on one of them like I'd had her in her kitchen back home.

I forced myself to push that thought out of my mind and leave the kitchen. Heading down another hallway, I passed through another large common area and two smaller rooms before getting to the wing of bedrooms. A small hallway led to six doors coming off a rounded vestibule. Each led into its own well-appointed bedroom, meaning there were enough for each of us to have our own, as well as Ethan when he arrived. That was nice because it meant there would be no awkwardness, and none of us had to worry about sharing our personal space with any of the others. At the same time, it did take some of the potential fun out of the giant slumber party set up for us here.

Jane and I couldn't sneak into each other's rooms if we were all literally off the same hallway. It was far easier to be discreet when there were hundreds of other people staying in the same place. And that was something I definitely wanted available to me. I hadn't been able to stop thinking about Jane and our night together since climbing out of her bed.

She laughed in one of the bedrooms, and I looked inside

to see her and Maddie sitting on the bed, engrossed in conversation with each other. She didn't even look my way. It was clear our night together didn't affect her in the same way. She wouldn't even acknowledge that anything happened and that didn't sit well with me.

CHAPTER 12

I was full of energy and excitement when we first got into the apartment. Being back in Paris and in the apartment in particular gave me a rush that was even stronger than I'd expected. It felt like a little piece of me I hadn't really let myself think about was finally in my grasp again. Even though I couldn't talk to any of the others about it or share any of the memories I had of this place, it felt amazing it just to be back. I could relish the familiarity and savor my favorite moments and memories within myself and feel happier than I had in a long time. Except for the night I'd spent with Nik.

Now, though, the adrenaline had worn off. Rather than just kicking back and relaxing to enjoy our first day in Paris, the team agreed to jump right into work. We didn't want the jet lag to take over and kill our productivity for the rest of the week. We'd been working for hours, trying to burn through the fatigue of our internal clocks being completely turned on their heads, but I could feel myself getting fuzzy, and I knew my brain was checking out of what was going on around me. I was only catching every few words everybody else was saying, and even the sketches I drew looked unfamiliar. Finally, I couldn't take it anymore. No amount of team spirit and morale was going to stop me from crashing. I stretched out on the couch where I'd dozed away many afternoons and quickly fell asleep.

I aimed for just a short nap, but I had no idea how long I was actually asleep when my eyes opened later. My body felt relaxed and my mind was refreshed, but it took me a few seconds for reality to set back in. It wasn't springtime in my younger years, and I wasn't here honing my paintings and savoring the beauty of the city. It was a totally different world now. The sun was starting to set, making the light in the room hazier and creating new shadows across the floor. The room was empty, and I didn't hear any voices in the apartment. Right before I'd fallen asleep, Maddie had mentioned wanting to go out into the city and start scouting locations. Somewhere in the back of my mind, I seemed to remember Toby suggesting he could go along with her. They must have decided to go, and Nik probably went with them, leaving me alone. I didn't mind. I was completely comfortable in the apartment and didn't need anybody there with me to feel secure.

I got up and wandered through the rooms, eventually ending up in the large dining room. I was surprised to find the table filled with food that wasn't there when I fell asleep. A baguette sat alongside a large basket of fresh fruit. A wooden board overflowed with what looked like a dozen varieties of cheese. A bottle of wine sat alongside a box tied with a gold ribbon. I knew that box. It was from one of my favorite chocolate shops right around the corner. I untied the ribbon and lifted the lid, eagerly dipping my fingers into the assortment of truffles inside.

"You found it."

Nik's voice startled me, and I whipped around, my fingers still in my mouth. I withdrew them and swallowed the bite of the truffle I took.

"You're still here," I said.

He gave a short laugh and strolled the rest of the way into the room.

"The others seemed like they would do just fine on their own, so I thought I'd hang out here." He looked at the table and the goodies displayed across it. "The landlady dropped this all off. She was asking after you."

I cringed slightly, feeling the stinging heat of a fierce blush rush across my cheeks. I'd really hoped Marguerite wouldn't bother us, considering how well she knew me.

"Wow. That is pretty exceptional customer service. I feel extremely welcomed. Do you feel welcomed?" I babbled, but Nik stopped me.

"I know you stayed here every spring since you turned eighteen," he said.

"You do?"

"Yes," he confirmed.

"Oh."

He walked up to the table and plucked a few grapes off the bunch in the bowl, tossing them into his mouth.

"She gave me quite the earful," he said.

"She did?"

This was not getting any better.

"Yes. She couldn't stop gushing about you and singing your praises. Probably because, according to her, you practically paid the mortgage on the building for the year when you came to stay for those three months each spring," Nik told me.

He picked up a small knife and sliced off a sliver of cheese, lifting his eyebrows at me with expectation.

"Would you believe I was a foreign exchange student?" I asked.

"Exchanged for what?" he asked, eating the slice and going for another handful of grapes.

"Um... baguettes?" My head dropped down. "Shit. All right." I lifted my head to look at him. "Here's the truth. I'm rich."

Nik burst into laughter. "That's the weakest confession anyone has ever given."

"I know. But here's the thing. I'm actually not. Not anymore, anyway," I continued.

"Am I safe to assume there's a story in there somewhere?" he asked.

"Yes," I said, dropping my head back and walking out of the dining room.

He followed behind me, and I went into the kitchen for a glass of water. Downing the glass in one swig, I set it in the sink and let out a resolute breath.

"Here we go. I used to be rich. This isn't a tragic 'my family was at the peak and is now in ruins' story. *They* are still wealthy. Very wealthy. That's how I know this place. They started bringing me to Paris when I was really young, and I fell in love with it, especially the art. I wanted to be surrounded by it and let it inspire me, so my mother and I would come for several weeks every year. When I got old enough, they started sending me on my own every spring. I would paint and draw, eat amazing food, and just wander around taking it all in," I told him, starting to feel nostalgic for those more carefree times.

"If this isn't a tragic story about how your family lost

everything and they are still wealthy, how did you end up only 'used to be rich'?" Nik asked.

I leaned my hip against the counter as I looked at him.

"That's my doing. They would like for me to still be wealthy, but only on their terms," I said.

"What do you mean?"

"They cut me off because they decided it was time for me to settle down, but I refused to marry the guy they want me to."

"What guy?" he asked.

"Preston Howell. Maybe you know him?" I asked.

Nik shook his head. "The name sounds vaguely familiar, but I don't know of him."

It confirmed what I assumed about Nik from the beginning. He was wealthy on a different level than even my family or the Howells. It could also mean he was what my parents would refer to, with a slight gasp and a lowered voice, as "new money." Either way, we didn't move in the same social circles.

"He was my neighbor growing up. My parents and his are close, and they got together and decided the world would be a lovely, shiny, homogenized place if they could combine their kingdoms with the betrothal of their children, which works in storybooks, but not so much in real life. Especially when one of those children has the silver spoon he was born holding in his mouth now shoved up his ass." I rubbed my eyes. "I probably could have gone for a little more decorum there."

"No," Nik said, shaking his head. "That pretty much summed it up. And trust me, I understand. It might not have gotten quite as far as being cut off, but I've had my fair share of people trying to control my life. Including thinking they know who would be best for me to marry. This also explains some things."

"Like what?" I asked.

"Why you don't know how to do anything," he said.

"This is literally my first job," I pointed out.

I was embarrassed, but he shook his head.

"You're doing great. You've gotten up to speed very quickly. I heard you even made some copies before we left," he said.

I laughed. "Thanks. It's my favorite new skill."

Our eyes met and the tension immediately started building between us. It heated up the kitchen and made every part of me tingle and ache. His pull was magnetic, and soon the desire was unbearable. Suddenly, I was in his arms and we were kissing frantically. I couldn't get close enough to him or kiss him deeply enough. My need was out of control, and I couldn't stop myself. Nik was just as desperate, his hands roving over me as his tongue tangled with mine.

I clawed at his shirt, yanking it out from the waistband of his pants. He pulled his mouth away from mine long enough to take his shirt off and toss it aside, then yank my mine off to join it. His skin against mine made my knees weak. I rose up on my toes to get closer to him, and he grabbed hold of my ass, using it to pull me hard against him. We kissed for another few hungry seconds before I stepped back away from him enough to reach for the button of his pants. I pulled the zipper down and shoved the pants down along with his boxers. Nik stepped out of them and unhooked my bra as I got rid of my own pants.

In a movement so fast and sudden it took my breath away, he grabbed me again and spun me around to face the island in the center of the kitchen. Stepping up behind me,

Nik used his knee to shift my legs apart a few inches. His hand pressed to the center of my back, pushing me forward. I stretched my arms out in front of me and grabbed onto the edge of the island, gripping it tightly as I felt his mouth touch my back between my shoulder blades. He kissed down my spine until he reached the small of my back, then drew his tongue back up in a long lick.

I was so ready for him the insides of my thighs were hot and wet, but Nik had something more planned for me. Lowering down to his knees behind me, he buried his face between my thighs and swept his tongue over my throbbing clit. I could barely hold myself up with the intense rush of pleasure, but used my fingers wrapped around the marble edge to keep me in place. My legs shook as he explored every fold and dip with his tongue, his fingers digging into my thighs. I arched my back to press harder against his mouth and was rewarded with his tongue plunging inside me. One arm wrapped around my hips, and his hand pressed to my lower stomach. It held me in place against his face, and seconds later, he turned it so he could massage my peak with the tip of his middle finger.

There was no way I was going to be able to take much of this, but I didn't want it to stop. The pleasure consumed me, taking complete control of my mind and body. I couldn't think of anything else but Nik and the incredible things he could do to my body. I didn't hold back. I gave myself over to every sensation, every delicious way he mastered me and made me his. Within seconds my body clenched and shuddered, and I screamed as a blinding climax tore through me.

Feeling Jane's climax shudder through her nearly did me in. I got to my feet as fast as I could and in one fast thrust sank my hard cock all the way into her. She cried out again and threw her head back as I filled her, and I leaned forward to stretch my body over her and kiss the side of her neck. She was so hot and wet, her body molding around me like we were crafted for this. I drew my hips back and gave another hard thrust forward, drawing another sound from her throat. That was all the slow and gradual I could manage.

Gripping her shoulder with one hand and her hip with the other, I slammed into her fast and hard. I was desperate for every slick inch of her body, every sound that bubbled up through her lips. Jane pushed up from lying flat on the island and pressed her hands to marble so she stood back against me. I wrapped my arm around her waist to hold her close and reached around with the other hand to dip my fingers between her thighs. Her hand reached up and dug into my hair, gripping it hard like she was trying to hold herself steady. She turned her head, and I met her mouth in a deep, seeking kiss.

Sweat was forming on our skin, and I let my hand slide against it to rise up to one breast. I held it, each hard thrust of my cock deep inside her making it bounce against my palm. Her nipple was hard and tight, and I swirled it between my fingers before moving my hand over to give the same attention to the other. Withdrawing from her, I turned her around and leaned her back against the island. Lowering to my knees in front of her, I drew one breast into my mouth. I swirled my tongue around it, then bit down lightly, drawing my teeth across it.

Massaging the other breast with my hand, I lowered my mouth down to kiss along the sweaty skin of her stomach. When I got to the valley between her hip bones, I eased her legs farther apart and swept my fingers through her lips to discover her dripping heat. She felt like silk on my fingertips, and I craved the taste of her. Her knees buckled when I tucked my head between her thighs and licked her. I pushed against her hip to hold her up and continued with my exploration until she pulled me away, gasping for breath.

I sat back and brought her down into my lap. Jane settled with her knees on either side of my hips and sank down onto me so I filled her again. This position put me at a different angle, and I savored being able to feel her in as many ways as possible. Her arms wrapped loosely around my neck, she leaned forward and caught my mouth. We kissed as I used one hand on the small of her back to grind her against me, and the other to push against the floor so I stayed as deep as possible.

Her hips rolling against me was intoxicating, and I broke the kiss so I could watch her. Without saying a word,

Jane gave me exactly what I wanted. Taking her arms from around my neck, she leaned back and supported herself on my lower legs. It gave me a full view of where our bodies came together and her breasts bouncing with her movements. I held on to her hips and eased her back and forth. Watching my cock slide in and out of her, glistening with the sweet wetness of her body, was almost unbearably sexy. I bit down on my bottom lip, not wanting it to end too soon.

I knew we could get caught at any moment. The others could walk back into the apartment and find us on the floor of the kitchen, but I didn't care that thought didn't deter me from wanting to stay buried inside Jane and keep worshipping every bit of her body. I couldn't help myself, not when it came to her. I could fight to keep myself under control and keep going for the rest of the evening.

But Jane knew exactly how to make that possibility obsolete. Her body still stretched out in front of me so I could watch every decadent, erotic movement, she took one hand from my leg and brought it between her thighs. Lifting her head to look right into my eyes, she slipped her fingertip down to gather some of her slickness from the shaft of my cock. Her lips parted in a silent gasp, and her eyes darkened into an even deeper slumbering stare when she settled her fingertip to her clit. It swirled in a tight circular motion, and her hips rocked harder in response to the layered sensation of me stroking inside her and her own hand.

Watching her sent a rush of more intense arousal through me. My entire body tensed and heated like it was going to burst into flames. I dug my fingertips harder into her hips and pounded faster. Jane gasped and whimpered, not holding back any of the intoxicating sounds. I groaned, gritting my teeth as I thrust harder. Her hand moved faster, and her eyes closed seconds before I felt her body tighten around me and a wave of spasms ripple along the length of my cock.

"Oh God Nik, yes, that feels so fucking good," she moaned.

I flipped Jane onto her back on the floor and pushed her thighs up with my arms. She held on to me, her fingernails clawing at my upper arms as I slammed into her at a frenzied pace. Her sounds rose up to screams as I rode her orgasm right into my own blistering finish. The roar that came out of me was primal, something from far down within me as I filled her with thread after thread of my seed, and I collapsed forward when it was over. She wrapped her arms around me, and I kissed her, pushing my hips forward so I stayed fully encased within her body to enjoy every lingering second of the intense pleasure she created. I couldn't catch my breath, I could barely see, but I wanted nothing more than that moment to keep going.

Almost as soon as her body stopped quivering and her breath had nearly returned to normal, Jane sat up and reached for her nearest article of clothing. Since it was her shirt, it didn't do her a lot of good. She looked around almost nervously until she spied her bra and scrambled over to it. I sat up much more casually and watched her hook her bra into place and adjust her swollen, still-pink breasts in the cups. She tugged her shirt down over it and then went on the search for where her panties landed. As she wriggled into them, I let out a short laugh.

"Should I be offended by how fast you're trying to put this behind you?" I asked. "I mean, I know I'm the one who slipped out on you last time, but I don't think you're going to be able to disappear that easily."

She shot me a look as she found her pants and stepped into them.

"I'm just trying to get dressed and presentable again as fast as I can. We have no idea when Maddie and Toby are going to walk back in here. And you never know, Ethan could have gotten an early flight and be here any minute," she said.

She sounded anxious, and I got up to start getting dressed. She was combing her fingers through her hair to try to neaten it again when I took a step toward her.

"Jane, we need to talk about what's happening," I said, dropping my shirt down over my head.

She shook her head like she was refusing the words before they got to her. Walking back over to the counter, she picked up the glass she'd set in the sink and filled it with water again.

"Nothing should be happening," she said.

She drank the water down quickly and set the glass aside, letting her head hang for a second.

"Why?" I asked. "Why should nothing be happening?"

I walked up behind her and put my hand on her back. She turned to face me, her eyes wide and filled with emotion. It was hard to decipher exactly how she was feeling and what was going through her mind, but somehow looking into the swirl of thoughts and emotions in her wide caramel-colored gaze told me so much of what we were going through was the same. It was hard to know what was going on in my mind and my heart, but I knew I didn't want to let it go.

"Because of our work relationship, Nik. Because of who you are and who I am. This might be my first job, but I know enough about the work environment to know this—" She gestured between the two of us. "—isn't appropriate."

I put my hands on her hips and pulled her closer to me, not wanting to lose the connection. This wasn't about sex or the way she woke up my body like no one ever had. In that moment I needed to touch her because of the way it made me feel. Being close to her reached something inside me I thought was gone. Maybe something I didn't even know was there.

"Fuck appropriate," I said. She scoffed and rolled her eyes, turning to try to get out of my hands, but I held her firm until she looked back into my eyes. "I'm serious. Fuck appropriate, Jane. This, what you and I have, isn't just some workplace fling. This could be real if we give ourselves the chance to find that out. I don't even know how to explain how you make me feel. You calm me down and excite me at the same time. You make me feel stronger, like I could take on the entire world for you, but I also feel like I can talk to you about anything. That's not something to just throw away."

"Nik, you're my boss. You're not some guy who works in the cubicle across the aisle, or a faceless vendor who some-times wanders through the office. You're in charge of the company I work for and constantly involved in my work and the work of the rest of the department. We're right there together all the time, affecting each other's work. There's a reason people say you shouldn't make the boardroom the bedroom," she said.

"I don't care what other people say. Let them do what they want. Let them ignore what they might have and throw it away because they want to only focus on their work. We don't have to do that. We don't have to answer to anyone else. If we're careful, if we don't let the personal interfere with the professional, this could work. The thing is, we're never going to find out if we don't try," I argued.

"And if we do try? If we try and it falls apart? Then what? What happens to the rest of the department? To the team and the work we're doing? How do we possibly keep working together after something like that?" she asked. "I just don't see how it's possible to completely separate those aspects of our lives and have it work."

I wanted to respond, but I heard the door to the apartment open and she rushed out. I followed after her, still unwilling to let go of this. She was so different, and I wasn't going to be able to just push that out of my mind. After my divorce I'd wanted nothing to do with relationships and thought there was no possibility of finding someone to share my life with. But that was different now. I was willing to try again for Jane.

CHAPTER 14

JANE

I couldn't believe the week in Paris was already almost over. It felt like we'd just gotten there, and I was starting to settle into the beauty and magic of the city when I realized it was already our last full day. I wanted it to linger and flow sweet and soft like the spring days and nights I used to spend there, but the intense schedule we'd been following didn't give us much of a chance for downtime and relaxation. Constant planning, strategizing, traveling, and shooting, not to mention the endless hours each evening looking through images, editing, and strategizing for the next day, ate up the days. Hours went by like minutes, and it felt like we had barely gotten the opportunity to even experience Paris. It was an absolute whirlwind, but even with the hectic schedule and hard work, I loved every minute of it.

I especially loved the minutes I'd spent wrapped in Nik's arms.

There hadn't been many of those minutes. The packed schedule and close proximity of the rooms in the apartment didn't give us any chance to be alone together. We hadn't touched each other since that first, frantic night, but that didn't stop me from fantasizing about him like crazy throughout the week. I'd never experienced anything even close to that night in the kitchen. It was desire and need like nothing I knew existed. It was like every part of me, mind, body, and heart, were reaching out for him and wouldn't be satisfied until we fully melded together. The passion was all-consuming, and I walked away from it feeling somehow changed, as if Nik had marked me as his.

The thoughts and memories were never far from my mind. No matter what we were doing or how hard we were working, all it took was hearing the sound of his voice or looking over at him. In that instant I was carried back to the kitchen and the way he took over my body. There was no hesitation, no cautious approach. He knew exactly what he wanted and claimed it powerfully while giving me more than I could have ever imagined. Every time I stepped into the shower in the bathroom attached to my room, I was extremely aware of his bedroom just on the other side of the wall. Every night when I went to bed, my mind was overrun with fantasies and dreams about him.

Nik hadn't said another word about our relationship since that night. I'd walked away from the kitchen with his words ringing in my head. He wanted more than just the incredible passion and intense pleasure we found in each other. He wanted to explore the possibility of what a real relationship could be, and the thought was both thrilling and terrifying. I didn't know how it could possibly fit into the reality of my new life, but even as I'd left the kitchen that first night, I knew the conversation would come back up. I was willing to try to talk it through and see what we could discover. Only, he never approached me again. There wasn't even a word.

I didn't know how to feel about it. Maybe all that talk about trying to pursue whatever was between us was just the heat of mystifying sex melting his brain, and when he'd calmed down it went away. Maybe all that really could exist between us was our undeniable chemistry and physical connection. All I knew was I wanted him again, no matter how inappropriate it was.

We saved the location I was most excited about for the final full day in the city. The scenic street right along the Seine was breathtakingly beautiful. It looked like we'd stepped into a painting and were wandering through the fantasy image exploring every idealist brushstroke and detail. I could imagine it exactly that way because I'd painted that very stretch many times before. That day, I wished I had my canvas and paints with me. I wanted to capture what was happening right then. I would have to settle for the shots for the print campaign we were there to get. The shots were turning out perfect, and some of the images we'd already captured were worthy of a gallery. I couldn't help but be proud as I watched the photographer and the models we hired to take the ideas we gave them and turn them into reality. The entire campaign was forming right in front of us, and it was turning out truly incredible.

I walked up behind Ethan where he sat at a computer monitor reviewing the pictures as the photographer took them. He pointed at a few and I nodded. We knew to say as little as possible. Talking or making comments about the pictures could completely throw off the photographer and the models. We needed to trust them to do their thing, and we'd take it from there. That's what editing was for, and the entire team knew we were looking at many long days and nights of working through the thousands of images ahead of us.

I stood back and reviewed more of the images. The entire effect was slick and edgy, but with the perfect hint of romance that made Paris the ideal choice. It was particularly appealing considering the feelings for Nik fluttering inside me. Out of the corner of my eye, I noticed him looking at me. Throughout the day he kept stealing glances at me and occasionally offering small, private smiles. I considered his words again. Maybe it wasn't just about our physical connection. Maybe he really did like me. And maybe he really did want more, but it was still my first job, one that was almost miraculous for me to find in the first place. There was little chance I'd ever find something else anywhere near like it and would end up having to accept something that didn't pay anywhere near as well and that didn't have anything to do with my art. I didn't know if I could risk that for a fling with my boss.

I glanced over again and saw Nik watching me. Maybe it wasn't a fling. Could he actually be serious about me?

That question tumbled through my mind for the rest of the day as we tried to squeeze every last drop out of the city. When we got back home and into the office, we would have a very limited time to tie up all the ends and get the campaign ready for launch. What we didn't capture now, we wouldn't have the chance to do again. So we spent every moment following every flight of fancy, every thought that popped into our minds. To one side, Maddie had a sound recorder set up. It constantly took in the audio of the area, including the people on the street, the soft sounds of the water, the photographer and models, and the team. We could use it later to enhance the video and add layers to the campaign. There was an amazing energy around us, fueling us to keep going even when we felt wrung out. Finally, there was nothing more we could do. The photographer took the last shot, we thanked the models and said goodbye, and it was over. I let out a breath, feeling both exhausted and invigorated, something close to having just ridden a massive roller coaster and trying to process it all once my feet were back on solid ground.

We all went back to the apartment to drop off the equipment and change out of the clothes we'd been wearing all day. Then it was time to actually spend a little bit of time enjoying the city. We walked out of the building, and I led the group to a café I always loved visiting. It wasn't the type of delicate, highly mannered little café many people think of when they think of Paris. Instead, it was a typical French local spot, filled to brimming with bright, colorful personalities and an energy that lit us all back up. We folded into the raucous atmosphere and found a table to sit down. It felt good to finally snag a few precious seconds to just relax and enjoy the experience of being there in the city. We watched the people go by and listened to snippets of conversations carried over to us by breeze scented like coffee and pastry.

After two cups of coffee, Nik looked at each of us.

"How about I bring everyone to dinner to celebrate the end of a successful shoot?" he asked.

"Um," both Maddie and Toby said at the same time.

They both kept their eyes down at the table like they were trying to think of something to say, then exchanged a glance. I didn't think they knew I caught the look they shared between them, and I had to wonder if there might be something going on between the head of the company and the assistant director of marketing. Something told me there were going to be a lot of conversations and maybe a few glasses of wine between Maddie and me when we got back to the office. I was happily open to hearing all about what was going on with her, but I was still reserved about Nik and me. I wasn't ready quite yet to talk about us and what was happening. Not until I knew what was really there and what it meant. There was no point in getting everybody involved and possibly changing the dynamic of the team in our work environment if nothing was going to come of it.

But the way Maddie and Toby looked at each other made me smile, and I looked forward to hearing more.

CHAPTER 15

I was doing the best I could to not stare at Jane while we were at the café. Going to the little spot tucked away off the beaten path was her idea. None of the others realized she had been here many times before and was familiar with the surroundings. She knew exactly the type of place it was and that if we wanted a taste of authentic Paris, and this was where we'd find it. Other places were set up and designed for the tourists who wanted to sit back in ornate wrought iron chairs and sip tiny cups of coffee while looking breezy and effortless. Many of them looked like they were constantly posing for pictures no one was taking. This café, though, was different.

There was an energy here that felt real and relaxed, like the people who came were absolutely comfortable. They weren't thinking about the tourists or feeling any type of expectation. They were just enjoying their time out with their friends. When we first walked in, it felt almost like we were infiltrating some secret realm, but we melded in and soon were laughing and talking with those around us who spoke English, or who were willing to speak it to us.

Jane was in her element. She sank right in, seamlessly finding her place again. It was like looking at her from her past. Rather than the woman coping with a massive shift in her life and trying to figure out who she was without the wealth and power of her family behind her, she was just Jane, living the life she always had. It brightened her face and awakened something inside her, making her even more beautiful. I didn't want the others to catch me staring at her, or to see the look in my eyes I was sure was there every time I did look her way. I had been thinking about her nonstop since the first night we were in Paris, but the thoughts went unfulfilled.

The week's schedule was crammed, and we were working like crazy to get our ambitious ideas for the shoot accomplished. It left no time to sneak off together. But that hadn't stopped me from jerking off every night to the memory of her and her incredible body christening that apartment kitchen. Sitting there in the café, I knew the memory was no longer enough. Just thinking about her and the way she felt wasn't going to get me through. I wanted her again, and I was going to find a way to make my desire a reality.

I invited the team to dinner to celebrate finishing the shoot, but they didn't respond as enthusiastically as I would have expected. Rather than immediately agreeing, Toby and Maddie exchanged an almost uncomfortable glance, then started making excuses.

"I'm not really all that hungry. Besides, I have some reading I need to catch up on." Toby looked at his phone. "Wow. I actually didn't realize how late it is. I need to get going."

His eyes flickered over to Maddie, then quickly away as he got up. She hopped to her feet a second later.

"Hold on. I'll share a cab with you. I'm headed that way for an appointment," she said.

I looked at them, confused by the excuses, but they didn't give me a chance to question them about it. Waving at Jane and me, they scurried off. I turned to Jane.

"He didn't say what direction he was going. How would Maddie know she was headed that direction?" I asked. "And come to think of it, what kind of appointment could she possibly have in the evening in a city she doesn't live in and has never visited?"

Rather than seeming as confused as I was, Jane giggled. She took a sip of the glass of wine she'd been babying since we got to the café and shook her head.

"I don't think she has an appointment," she said. "And any direction Toby is going, she is headed that way, too."

"What do you mean?" I asked.

"I think Toby and Maddie might be succumbing to the magic of Paris. Haven't you noticed the way the two of them have been looking at each other? They have gotten mighty close since we've been here. Suddenly Ethan doesn't seem all that important, and Toby is going to Maddie for every-thing. He's been getting her opinion about all the shoots, and there has been a whole lot more giggling going on between the two of them than I think pictures of models on a fountain really warrants," she told me.

"You know, that makes sense. I've noticed them being a lot closer than usual, too." I grinned at her. "I guess we aren't the only ones taken by the City of Lights."

Jane smiled but turned her eyes down. I chuckled and tossed some money onto the middle of the table to pay for what we'd ordered, then stood up, reaching for her hand.

"Let's go take a walk," I suggested.

"A walk?" she asked, putting her hand in mine and letting me help her to her feet.

"Yes," I said, laughing softly. "A walk. Isn't that what people do in Paris? We can enjoy the evening air. Look at the lights."

Maddie and Toby took off in the opposite direction as the house, likely heading off for a romantic evening, enjoying the last of their time in Paris, but that meant they weren't going to be in the apartment. Now that I knew Jane and I would have it all to ourselves with little chance of them suddenly returning, I was fully bent on seducing her.

"That sounds lovely," Jane answered.

We started away from the café, but I stopped.

"Actually, give me just a second. I'll be right back," I told her.

Leaving her at the table, I make a beeline for the restroom. I was a few yards away when I noticed Jane was no longer waiting alone. She was sitting back in her seat, but the one I'd occupied just a few minutes before now had another man in it.

He sat near the edge of his seat, leaning toward Jane as he spoke to her in rapid French. I couldn't understand a word he was saying, but it was obvious Jane did. She sat back in her chair casually, a bemused smile on her face. Every few seconds, she gave a slow nod, then responded in comfortable, fluent French. I walked up to the side of the table and stared down at the man and Jane.

"What's going on?" I demanded a little more harshly than was probably warranted.

Jane laughed and gestured toward the man, who looked up at me, then back to her, rolling his eyes.

"This guy is hitting on me," she explained.

I took a step so the man had to see me.

"Conversation is over, buddy. Why don't you go take a walk?" I said.

The man didn't even look at me. Instead, he shifted farther to the edge of the chair and leaned closer to Jane. He slid his hands across the table toward her and continued speaking, his voice lowering slightly. She tilted her head to the side and narrowed her eyes, her eyebrows knitting together as if something he rambled at her was offensive. She replied, and he chuckled in a self-congratulatory, arrogant way. His hand lifted toward her like he was going to brush a strand of hair away from the side of her face. I wasn't about to let him touch her.

Grabbing the back of the chair, I gave it a firm yank. It pulled the chair right out from under the Frenchman, spilling him right out onto the ground. Jane laughed and jumped to her feet. The man wasn't nearly as amused when he stood. His eyes burning into me now, he started yelling and gesturing wildly. I still couldn't understand what he was saying, but I could recognize belligerence no matter what language it was in. He was clearly not happy about my interference in his attempt to woo Jane and wanted to save face by fighting back. He lunged at me, and I ducked at the clumsy attempt at punching me.

Jane could see what was happening and interjected herself before anything could escalate. Grabbing my arm, she threw a look over her shoulder at the man and spat something in French. She dragged me out of the café and didn't stop until we were a block away and could no longer hear the man screaming. She released my arm and let out an exasperated sigh.

"What?" I asked.

"Did you really have to do that?" she asked.

"What do you mean? He's the one who came after me," I told her.

"Yeah, after you dumped him out of his chair onto the ground," she pointed out.

"Technically, it was my chair," I corrected. "He was just sitting in it trying to take liberties with you."

She stared at me for a few seconds, and then her face cracked into a smile and she started laughing.

"Trying to take liberties with me?" she asked when she could finally catch her breath.

"What?" I asked, feeling slightly defensive at her reaction.

Jane shook her head.

"I'm sorry. You're right. He was absolutely out of line. He should have known to leave his calling card and wait for the appropriate moment when my chaperone would allow him to come visit," she said, the laughter tumbling out of her all over again.

A smile tugged at my lips.

"Are you making some sort of commentary about me?" I teased.

She shrugged playfully. "Maybe I am."

"Well, personally, I just thought I was blending in. You went to all the trouble of bringing us to a spot where the tourists don't go. I figured I would show them just how welcomed I feel by the locals," I said.

Jane rolled her eyes and made a snorting sound, but she was still smiling.

"I'm sure that man will remember your demonstration of goodwill and diplomacy for a long time," she told me.

"I hope so. Then maybe next time he'll know better than to..." My voice trailed off as I tried to figure out how to finish that sentence without letting the possessive feeling I had toward Jane became too obvious.

I didn't know how she would react and didn't want to ruin the fun, airy mood that was finally between us after a week of having to stay away from each other because the rest of the team was too close.

"Try to take liberties with a woman?" she asked.

The tone in her voice was slightly different now. Some of the teasing was gone, and it was like she was trying to say something else but didn't know exactly what words to say.

"I don't care what he does with just any woman. I just don't want him doing anything with you," I told her.

She offered me a smile, and her eyes said that smile was just for me. My jealousy faded away, and I reached down to take her hand. Her fingers intertwined with mine, and we walked slowly along the street.

CHAPTER 16

I felt so comfortable with Nik, so at ease. It wasn't anything I would have expected. When we first started talking about coming to Paris, I didn't know what it would be like. I knew what to expect of the city, of course, but I didn't know what it was going to be like to be there with him. I didn't know if I'd be able to stand being so close to him in a place linked with romance and seduction. It was even more difficult after our first night together. I craved more of him, more than I ever wanted something in my entire life. But we'd left the conversation about our potential relationship at such an odd place. It made everything feel off-balance, almost tenuous, like either one of us could make or break the situation with a single word. In all honesty, I expected more of the "break."

As much as I wanted to pretend that we could just put the entire situation behind us and pretend it didn't happen, that wasn't realistic. Something that incredible and impactful left a mark. We couldn't just skim over it and spend the rest of the week acting like we were just colleagues. Every time we were in the same room together, it heated up. Every time we spoke, my heart beat just a little bit faster. I never stopped wanting him to touch me. I never stopped wanting to kiss him and feel his body against mine. But in that moment, when he took my hand and we started walking, I realized there was more than that.

I didn't just want Nik. I wanted to be near Nik. I felt good around him. He made me laugh, and I felt like I could be myself around him, which led me immediately to the feeling that maybe I was making a mistake. I was letting myself get too cozy and not keeping my eyes on the bigger picture. He squeezed my hand and guided me a little closer. We turned to each other and shared a smile. The magical romance of Paris was definitely in the air that night. I let myself relax, telling myself it wasn't a mistake. Not really. I liked Nik, and he was proving to be wonderful company on such a magical night. Far better company than I would have imagined even just before we left to come here. I didn't want to push that away just for the worry of what was going to happen next.

"Have you enjoyed being in Paris?" I asked.

"Yes," Nik told me. "Some parts of it more than others."

I slid my eyes over to him and noticed a hint of a smile on his lips, but he was still looking directly ahead.

"I think the shoots for the campaign have been very successful."

"Not the most successful part of this trip, but I'll take it," he said.

He was being clever, and I decided to play along.

"Oh, really? There's a part of it you think was more successful?" I asked.

"Absolutely," he said, then shrugged. "But I might be wrong."

That stung a little. "What?"

"Yeah. I might just be remembering it as more successful than it was because of the circumstances."

"The circumstances?" I asked.

"You know, jet lag, the adrenaline of getting here, the surroundings. My opinion could be swayed. It's like trying to determine if a marketing campaign worked just because of one person's opinion. I need more information."

That brought the smile back to my lips.

"More information, huh?" I asked.

Nik pulled me a little closer. "Definitely more. I need some real perspective. I might just need to stay up all night going over everything in very close detail. I wouldn't want to miss anything."

"That sounds like a lot of work," I commented. "Must be so hard."

He was trying to seduce me, but maybe, just maybe, I was trying to seduce him back. The tension between us was ramping up. I was extremely aware of the feeling of his hand in mine and our skin against each other. The heat of his body next to me stood out against the softness of the evening, and I felt the intense pull toward him. The heat and need were building up stronger with every step. It felt like at any second we weren't going to be able to bear just walking alongside each other. Just like he'd picked me up and put me on the island in the kitchen, he was going to bring me into one of the alleys and take me right up against the wall.

I might even let him.

Fortunately, or possibly unfortunately depending on how I was going to look at it, it didn't have to come to that. When I looked up and started paying attention to where we were, I realized we had walked all the way back to the apartment. I was so wrapped up in Nik and enjoying being there beside him, I hadn't even realized he'd led us back through the narrow streets and to the unmarked door. It seemed ridiculous when I thought about it, but that door was one of my favorite things about coming back to Paris. Every spring while I was anticipating my return, I thought about that door. It wasn't anything like most people would think of when dreaming of their fantasy stay in the city. It was small and nondescript. Nothing marked it or gave any indication of what was waiting just beyond. I loved that about it. It felt like my own little secret.

And now I got to share it with Nik.

We walked into the building and up to the door that led inside. Nik walked into the kitchen and came back with a bottle of wine and a corkscrew. He set the bottle down on the side table, and I crossed to the old record player against the wall. Like most of the books filling the shelves, the player had been sitting in the apartment for decades and was a part of my oldest memories of Paris. I flipped through the records and chose one, settling it into place and setting the needle on it. There were a few seconds of awkward scratching and white noise, and then the apartment filled with an old, slow, romantic song. I sighed and let my eyes close for a moment, just to enjoy the sound of the music.

I heard the wine open and turned to watch Nik pour it into two glasses. He picked them up and carried them over to me, holding one out.

"Are you sure you trust me with this?" I asked, looking at him through my lowered eyelashes. "You know how I get with wine."

It seemed like that first night we were together, after he'd brought me to dinner when we'd stayed late at the office, was forever ago. Paris and perspective gave us distance.

"I know exactly how you get with wine," Nik said, his voice dipping lower and turning velvety.

Tipping the glass against my lips, I took a sip. It was like his voice, smooth and rich, going straight to my head.

"Are you ready to go back?" I asked. "For your Paris adventure to be over?"

"I don't want to think about that," he said. "Not right now. Tonight, I only want to think about you."

We each took another sip of wine, and Nik took my glass from my hand. He set them both down on the table and came back to me. Taking my hand, he led me over to the open area of the floor where the lights of the city outside spilled from the window and drew me into his arms. I breathed in the warm, spicy, clean smell of him and relaxed into the warmth of his chest. One hand settled on my hip while the other took one of mine.

I couldn't remember the last time I'd danced like this. I didn't know if I ever had. There had been times when I'd danced with men, of course. Even slow danced. The events and galas that dotted my life before the great break with my parents always involved dancing, but it was never like this. I'd never had a man cradle me in his arms like something both precious and desirable, and I never wanted to just melt into a dance partner and let the music take over.

The dance was slow and sensual. We were barely moving, yet it was lighting my body on fire. We pressed together, our hips swaying, our hearts beating against each other. Nik ducked his head down to lean his face against the side of mine, and I felt his breath on my neck. My hand slid out of his and ran down his arm to rest on his shoulder, and then I looped both around his neck. His hands slipped around my hips and settled onto the small of my back and held me closer.

Nik's lips brushed along my collarbone and up my neck. It wasn't a kiss as much as it was him breathing me in, cherishing me with just that soft touch. Finally, his lips made it up to mine and he kissed me. It was that simple and that intense at the same time. His mouth settled onto mine, and my heart rejoiced. I'd been longing for that kiss. All week I'd waited for Nik to kiss me again, and finally he had. There might have been questions in my mind before, but they were gone now. At least, I'd decided to push them away and not let myself dwell on them. The magic of Paris was flowing, and I figured I might as well enjoy it.

Maybe it would all change when we got back to New York, but for now, this was the moment I was living. And I wanted to live it to its absolute fullest.

The kiss deepened, and I succumbed to the desire. We stopped moving and concentrated on kissing. There wasn't the same frantic desperation this time. We had the apartment to ourselves and could take all the time we wanted. Instead, the kiss was deep and seeking. There was more behind it than just the tension between us breaking. Instead, we took the time to feel each other's lips and the touch of our tongues. I moaned softly as Nik nibbled at my bottom lip, then swept his tongue across it. My hands moved from being wrapped around his neck to sliding up to the back of his head so my fingers dug into his hair. He looped one arm around my waist, and the other hand ran up the back of my neck and held me.

We moved in tandem, kicking off our shoes and reaching for each other's clothes. Little by little, I revealed his skin. I didn't tear away his shirt or shove his pants out of place. I reverently released each button and slid my hands over his shoulders to ease the fabric away, guiding it off his hands and finally letting it drop. Brushing my lips along his skin, I lowered myself down to my knees and opened his pants. I tucked my fingers into the waistband of his pants and boxers and brought them down, helping him step out of them. Staying in place, I slipped out of my pants and shirt, leaving only my black lingerie. When I'd put it on that morning, it had been for him. I didn't know he would see it, but somehow, I wanted him to feel it, but it was so much better knowing he would see the delicate panties and low-cut bra.

When he was bare, I ran my hands up Nik's legs and tucked my head forward to draw my tongue up the underside of his erection in one long lick. He drew in a shuddering breath. I wanted to savor him, to memorize his feeling on my lips and tongue. I moved slowly, not rushing or hurrying past any moment we had together. He stood still, his hands resting on mine on his thighs, and breathed.

CHAPTER 17

NIK

"Holy fuck, that feels incredible," I breathed as Jane's tongue swirled expertly along my cock.

Jane enveloped me, enraptured me. The way she touched me made the rest of the world disappear around me, and all I could think about—all I wanted to think about—was her and the way she made me feel. Her mouth played across my hard cock both passionately and tenderly. She traced her tongue around the edge of the head, concentrating the tip on the bundle of nerves on the underside. It sent a shiver through me and I groaned, my head falling back and my eyes closing. After a few moments of the intense worship, Jane stood up and stepped up against me.

I took her into my arms, dipping my head to kiss her again. Gathering up our clothes, I took her hand and silently led her to the back of the apartment and into my bedroom. Even though it was only us home at the moment, I closed the door behind us. I wanted the privacy of our own space, closed off from everything and everyone else.

We met in the middle of the room, and I gathered her

into my arms again. I dipped my head down to bury my face between her breasts. Her skin was so soft and smooth against mine, and smelled sweet, like a combination of soap and roses. But there was something else there, just beneath the surface, something musky, warm, and distinctly Jane.

One of the many things I adored about Jane was that she always wore lingerie. I didn't always get to see it, but the times I had the chance to peel away her clothes and reveal what she had hidden underneath I discovered lace, satin, and silk. She was a pure confection, decadent and luscious, and wearing lingerie even when she topped it with jeans and a T-shirt only enhanced that. And on that day it was black and very brief, concealing almost nothing, and yet what little it did cover elevated the sexiness. I didn't want to take it away too soon. Instead, I brushed my mouth over the see-through black cups and swept my tongue beneath the fabric to flick across her nipple. The clasp was at the front of her bra, and I finally released it, allowing the delicate cups to fall away from her skin. As they did, I took one breast in my mouth and the other in my hand. My other hand pressed against the small of her back, holding her close.

"You are so damn beautiful," I told her.

We moved slowly together toward the bed as I slipped the straps of her bra back off her arms and let it fall to the floor. When the backs of her thighs hit the mattress, Jane sat, and I used my arm around her waist to lift her and ease her backward toward the head of the bed. She stretched out luxuriously across the bedspread, not trying to hide anything from me. I loved the way she did that. She was on display for me, not holding back or trying to keep anything away. I sat on my knees and looked at her, just enjoying the view of her kiss-reddened lips, sultry caramel eyes, and long red hair strewn across the pillow. She was perfection, and I felt a surge of pride at being the one to have the privilege to touch her.

"So beautiful," I repeated.

Jane opened her arms to me, and I climbed over to come down on top of her. My body settled over hers, pressing her down into the mattress, and she let out a happy sound. She lifted her head to touch her mouth to mine, and I caught hers in a kiss as I reached down to wriggle her panties away. Her thighs parted and my hips settled between them. Jane drew in a breath when the tip of my cock slid down her slick center and found her opening. Pulling away from the kiss, I looked down into her face. Her eyes opened and she didn't take them away from mine as she slowly pressed her hips forward to ease me inside.

"I need you Nik," she whispered.

I met her hips and sank into her. She welcomed me easily, her body forming around mine readily. We were learning each other in every way possible, and it only intensified the incredible chemistry and bond we found in each other. I filled her as deeply as I could and held still, just wanting to feel her wrapped around me.

"Perfect," I sighed.

After a few seconds staying in that position, Jane ran her hands down to my hips and nudged them, guiding me into smooth, slow strokes inside her. She lifted her legs and wrapped them around my waist, tightening the connection of our bodies. I rocked my hips against her, moving inside her without our bodies separating. Our pace was slow, but the intensity built quickly. Moving slowly and focusing on every sensation allowed me to truly feel every bit of her and give my body over to her as much as she was giving herself over to me. We kissed deeply, our tongues slipping across each other and my teeth nipping at her bottom lip.

I was nearly overwhelmed. It was unlike anything I'd ever experienced. My mind and body connected, each spiraling into new, undiscovered realms of excitement and pleasure. Every tiny sound she made, every time her lips touched mine or her hand slid across my skin, it grew stronger. I'd never felt this way about a woman before. I was changed by her, and there was nothing that would ever change me back.

My orgasm hit me powerfully, washing over me in a sudden wave that took my breath away. I clung hard to Jane, feeling her body responding to mine and her heart pounding against my chest. She gasped and cried out, kissing my shoulder and pressing her hands into my back as her pussy spasmed around me and milked every last ounce of my seed from my body. We held each other tightly as we rode through the surges of sweet, delirious sensation. I slid over to my side and gathered her against me, holding her close.

As I lay there holding Jane in my arms, I knew I'd never get enough. Nothing would ever be able to compare to her sweet, soft body curled up in the crook of my side, her head resting on my chest. My fingers trailed up and down her back and along the curve of her hip as her skin cooled down and her body relaxed. Her breathing slowed and a soft sound like a gentle coo told me she was asleep. I considered just reaching down for the blankets, pulling them up over us, and falling asleep right along beside her. She could stay the night there in my arms rather than having to move. It sounded amazing.

She seemed so peaceful and comfortable I didn't want to wake her up and make her move back into her room. But it was more than that. I wanted her there. With every part of me and every ounce of my being, I wanted to keep holding her. Maybe forever. In the short time I'd known Jane, I had become addicted to her. Even spending a few hours apart asleep in different beds seemed like far too much for me. I didn't want her out of arms reach for more than a few minutes. I wanted to know what it was like to wake up in the morning and look over to see her face. I wanted to kiss her good morning before I even spoke a word. If we woke up early enough, I wanted to sink into her again and welcome the day with our own private celebration.

But that wasn't an option, and I knew it. No matter how much I wanted to keep her there with me and not let her out of my sight or my arms until morning, that wasn't the time or place for it. I had to force myself to remember the world still did exist around us. Even if it felt like we were the only two people and nothing else mattered, there were still other people staying at the apartment. Ethan had to hop on the earliest plane he could as soon as we finished shooting to get back to the office for another meeting before jumping on the editing, but that still left Maddie and Toby to come invade our space. They would likely be out most of the night, but when they did come back, they would notice if Jane's bedroom was suspiciously empty and we both came out of mine the next morning. I didn't want to expose her to any sort of sordid speculation.

With the hesitation she expressed, I knew Jane would be absolutely mortified if the others found out about our relationship that way. It would be embarrassing just from a personal perspective, but she would also be terrified it would make an irreversible swing to the dynamic of our team. We had to be more careful than that and take our time figuring out what this all meant. And that meant not being able to really spend the night with her. Not yet, anyway.

Taking just a few more seconds to relish holding her close, I carefully slid away from Jane and scooped her into my arms. I carried her through the small round end of the hallway where all the bedroom doors opened and brought her into her room. Supporting her with my arm, I pulled back the covers and settled her between the sheets. She let out a contented sigh as I tucked the blankets around her again and leaned down to kiss her gently.

"Good night," I whispered.

I walked back to my room and got back into bed. It still felt warm and smelled like her. As I lay there staring up at the ceiling, satisfied and relaxed but not able to sleep, I couldn't stop thinking about Jane and what I saw for us. This couldn't end here. This wasn't just some fling brought on by the lights and romance of Paris. There was so much more to it, there had to be, we just didn't have words for it. Yet, that was the important part. It was time to find those words and make things permanent with Jane. I wasn't going to waste any time or let the opportunity slip past me.

As soon as we got back to Manhattan and I had the chance to spend some time with her without the rest of the team breathing down our necks, I was going to talk to her about us. I needed to tell her I wanted her. Not as an employee, not as just someone to have around who kept me entertained and who I could have a fling with whenever the chance showed itself. I wanted her as my partner. It was time for us to talk about ourselves and establish a real relationship we could bring out into the rest of the world. She might be hesitant at first. In fact, I was fairly well sure she wasn't going to just immediately jump into agreeing with me. But that didn't deter me. I was confident I could convince her to give me a chance, to give us a chance.

Coming to that conclusion brought a strange sense of peace over me. Folding my hands behind my head, I sank into the pillows and thought about how much things had changed. Reflecting on why Jane and our relationship was so important to me now, I couldn't help but notice how much my priorities shifted when I met her. For so many years I worked hard to build up my business. I put all my time, energy, and effort into shepherding my investments until I accomplished the success I had. My whole life I knew what I wanted, and that was the type of money, power, and prestige I achieved. I finally felt like I could take a step back from that and put my focus on something other than building my empire.

I wasn't going to make the same mistakes this time. Not with Jane. I wasn't going to let myself fall into the same traps and do the same things I did during my marriage to my ex-wife, Angela. But it wasn't just my change of perspective that made me sure that wasn't going to happen. Jane was nothing like Angela and the person she turned out to be. She was something completely different, and I felt like that was exactly what I needed. I closed my eyes and let myself drift to sleep with a smile on my face, slipping into a dream of my life with Jane.

CHAPTER 18

JANE

There's a lot to be said for the power of adrenaline and its ability to carry you through a challenging task. But adrenaline can only get you but so far, as I quickly learned after getting home from Paris. We knew before leaving for the trip it wasn't going to be a leisurely visit to the city. Only having a week there meant having to fill every available moment with as much work as possible. Whenever there was enough light to shoot, we were on location with the photographer and models. If we weren't actively shooting, we were scouting out the next place we wanted to shoot, going to the appropriate authorities to get permission to use the locations, and going through what we'd shot for the day. It left little to no downtime. We barely even stopped to eat, sometimes trying to stuff food in our mouths as we traveled from place to place.

But we got through it thanks to the adrenaline that kept our energy flowing right up until the moment I got onto the plane from France to New York. It was as if as soon as I sat down, the seat absorbed the last remaining fragments of my energy and there was absolutely nothing left. I wanted to curl up in Nik's arms and let him cradle me as I slept like the night before. I hated waking up in my bed without him there beside me. There were a few strange moments of wondering if I had dreamed up the entire interaction. I distinctly remembered falling asleep in Nik's room, but woke up alone in my own. But after those first few seconds, I knew it wasn't a dream.

We didn't get any time to really talk, but he slipped into my room and handed me the clothes I'd left behind, explaining he brought me in after I fell asleep. It was so sweet of him, wanting to protect me and stop the others from discovering us together. At the same time, I wished for those hours in his arms. And I wished for them again when I curled up to sleep in the plane. His seat was right beside mine, but I had to keep myself from tipping over onto his chest the way I wanted to.

My energy didn't get better once we got back to Manhattan. If anything, stepping back into the sardine can of my apartment after spending the glorious week in the sprawling Paris rental fatigued me even more. Fortunately, Nik timed the trip perfectly, so we arrived back in New York on Friday evening. It gave us the entire weekend to recover from jet lag and the adrenaline crash. For me, that meant becoming a hermit for the weekend. I turned off my phone and tried to reset my sleep cycle by essentially sleeping around the clock. It probably wasn't the best method, but it worked out. By the time I woke up Monday morning, I felt human again.

But the world had definitely gone on without me. Turning on my phone revealed a series of missed text messages and several missed calls, including a few from an unknown number. A few too many presses of the snooze button meant I didn't have the time to scrutinize the texts or my voicemail before leaving for work. But as soon as I took a spot on the subway, I listened to my messages. I immediately lit up when I heard Nik's voice. Ducking my head so no one around me would see the smile on my face that was way too enthusiastic for early Monday morning on the subway, I listened to it again.

The message was a little bit awkward, but that just made it better. Nik, the powerful alpha who made my knees weak and could make people do anything he wanted with little more than a look, sounded almost nervous. He finally pieced together an invitation to dinner.

On Saturday. Damn it.

I was instantly disappointed I missed the message during my self-imposed hiatus from participation in the world around me. Not seeing Nik for more than two days was hard on me. Much harder than I would have ever expected. I missed him. Even though I'd just seen him Friday night when he'd brought me home from the airport and made sure I was settled in. And even though we spent the last week living in the same apartment. I just couldn't seem to get enough of him.

Even through my disappointment, the message gave me a boost. It meant he was actually into me. I listened to the message one more time before getting to my stop. Tucking my phone away in my purse, I walked toward the office at a faster clip than usual. I was excited to get to work and see what the day had ahead for me.

Before I even got all the way into my office, my smile got even bigger. Sitting on my desk was a large flower arrangement. Setting my purse and bag aside, I plucked the card from within the blooms.

Here's to taking liberties.

There was no signature on the card, but there didn't need to be. I laughed softly at the memory of my conversation with Nik on our romantic walk through Paris. My smile got so big my cheeks ached. I didn't think I could feel any happier. Unless I was near Nik. And that's exactly what I wanted to do.

Taking the note with me, I walked out of my office and headed toward Nik's. The receptionist he'd brought in during his second week and planted in front of his commandeered space was known throughout the building. She didn't let anyone just go see Nik. If you didn't have an appointment, you didn't go in. Unless, of course, you knew how to sneak by her. At the moment I approached she was distracted by something in her purse, and I didn't hesitate to take advantage of the opportunity. Rushing past her, I sneaked up to Nik's door and opened it. But when I slipped in and turned to thank Nik for the flowers, I didn't get the welcome I expected.

Nik wasn't alone. He was sitting on the couch next to a beautiful blonde woman, their heads held close together as they spoke quietly.

"Oh," I said, shocked by the unexpected woman.

The card slipped from my hand and fluttered to the ground. They turned to look at me, and the withering look in her eyes made me want to disappear.

"Hello," she said in a chilly voice.

"I'm sorry," I said. "I didn't realize you were busy. I just came in to... you know what, it's not important."

"Who are you?" the woman asked.

In any other circumstances, I'd be offended, but the sheer surprise and painful hit of emotion in my heart took away any chance of a witty retort. Or any retort. I stood there silently, staring at her and Nik, trying to talk myself into believing some sort of logical explanation. Nik looked between the two of us a few times, then gestured toward me.

"She's an employee. This is Jane, my new marketing assistant," he said.

I didn't think the pain in my heart could get worse, but that proved me wrong. I nodded through the searing ache set in place by him referring to me in such a cold, generic way.

"Hello," I managed to force out.

"Jane, this is Angela. My ex-wife."

My jaw dropped, but I brought it back up as fast as I could. All I could think was a plea to the universe not to throw up right there in the office. Tears stung in my eyes, but I refused to let them out.

"Lovely to meet you," I said, glancing her way as briefly as possible before looking back at Nik. "I just came by to remind you about the meeting this afternoon."

Nik nodded. "Thank you, Jane. I'll see you later."

It was a dismissal. He had no more need for me. I reached down for the note and left, closing the door behind me.

"How did you get in there?" the receptionist demanded, but I ignored her.

I wandered back to my office in a fog. By the time I got there and shut the door behind me, I was still unsure what had just happened. That couldn't possibly have been Nik cozied up to another woman first thing in the morning. Not just another woman. His ex-wife. A woman he was married to at some point. I dropped down in my chair and called Elly. I needed an emergency girls' lunch to talk this out.

Part of me expected Nik to come to my office at some point during the day and give me an explanation, but by lunch, there'd been no word from him. I moved the flower arrangement down onto the floor behind my desk. I didn't want to throw it away, but I also didn't want it sitting there in my face all day. The second I walked into the restaurant and sat across from Elly, she could tell something was wrong.

"Oh, no. What happened?" she asked.

Deciding she needed the full story to have a proper perspective on the situation, I went backward.

"Remember how I told you the marketing team needed to go to Paris for a shoot?" I asked.

"Yes. And I also remember asking you to call me when you got back and let me know how it went. Didn't hear from you. Just putting that out there," she said.

"I'm sorry. I meant to call. Really, I did. It was an exhausting week. When I got home, I just completely crashed and basically slept the entire weekend. But wait a minute, go back to the trip," I told her.

I gave her the rundown of the time I spent with Nik in Paris and paused for her response.

"What happened to pretending the first time didn't happen?" she asked.

I knew that was coming.

"That plan doesn't work after the second time. Or the third. But here's the thing. He said he wants us to be together. Like, actually together. He said we could figure out the professional side of it and everything would work out," I told her.

"That's wonderful," Elly replied, then hesitated when I didn't immediately jump in to join her excitement and instead stuffed a French fry in my mouth. "Isn't it?"

"You would think," I said, swallowing my bite. "And this morning I found a voicemail from him I missed asking me to dinner Saturday; then there was a flower arrangement from him waiting on my desk when I got to the office."

"Why do I have the feeling this story is about to take an unexpected and probably not happy twist?" she asked.

I let out a sigh.

"What do you know about Angela?" I asked.

"Angela?" she asked.

"Yes. Nik's ex-wife," I told her.

Elly nodded. "Devin mentioned his divorce a few times. Apparently, it was pretty hard on him. Nik hasn't really dated anyone since."

"Maybe that's because the women who think they're dating him keep finding him cuddled up on the couch with her," I suggested.

Elly stared at me from across the table, and I explained what happened.

"I'm sorry, Jane," she said. "You haven't heard anything from him?"

"No."

"I'm sure you will. There has to be some sort of an explanation. It can't be as bad as you're thinking."

I tried to agree, but it didn't feel genuine. We finished lunch, our conversation moving to the baby coming and my plans to do some baby shopping with her, and I headed back to the office. I got back just in time to go into the conference room for the meeting with Ethan, Toby, Maddie, and Nik. He was late coming in and when he arrived, he didn't even look in my direction. He seemed distracted, and I couldn't help but wonder what happened after I left his office that morning.

CHAPTER 19

NIK

G oddamn it.

I couldn't get my thoughts straight. My brain felt like it was spinning, and I couldn't make it settle down enough to actually focus on one train of thought. Which, at that moment, should have been the meeting going on around me. I had been distracted since Angela left. Seeing her was the last thing I'd expected to happen to me that day. All weekend my mind had only been on Jane. I couldn't stop thinking about her and what went on between us in Paris. We still hadn't been able to talk about us or our future since leaving our business trip. Even the long flight home from France hadn't afforded us much in the way of privacy. When we had that talk, I wanted it to be just the two of us, away from everything and everyone else, and able to express everything we were thinking and feeling. That's why I'd called her on Saturday, inviting her to dinner.

It was disappointing when she didn't answer or call me back, but I understood. She'd seemed nothing short of exhausted when I'd dropped her off from the airport. I could only imagine she was taking the days before heading back to the office as a chance to recharge. It only made me miss her more. The flowers I ordered to be waiting on her desk for her when she arrived were meant to be the opening salvo, the introduction to what I hoped would be a life-changing conversation for both of us.

Of course, I ordered them before my receptionist announced I had a visitor and I looked up to see Angela walk into my office. To say having her there was tense would be a tremendous understatement. With the exception of a few inconvenient brushes and accidental encounters over the years, the last time we'd seen each other was when she walked out on me. Ten years ago, she told me she never wanted to see me again. In her words, she was marrying a man so rich, he had his own zip code and had no need of me.

I'd resented her at the time. Still building my business and pushing myself every second of my life to achieve my goals, I felt like she'd betrayed me. Knowing she'd cheated on me was salt in an open wound. It took time for me to come to terms with the reality that all that work, and the time spent away from her was part of what drove her into the arms of that other man. Not that it gave her a pass, but it was enough to make me feel guilty.

That same guilt was what made me push through the shock of seeing her again this morning and let her come in to talk to me. It was also the same guilt that came rushing back even stronger when Angela burst into tears and told me she was getting another divorce. Tears streamed down her face, and she gasped for breath, nearly losing control as she told me about the slimy man who'd prepared to leave her for months as she just went along thinking everything was perfect. He'd managed to hide most of his assets so she wouldn't be able to access them in the divorce, then simply called her one day while she was out shopping and announced their marriage was over. He'd had the locks changed before she got home. The hidden assets combined with their prenuptial agreement and the fact that she never gave him any children meant he cast her out basically penniless.

I had to admit there were a few moments during the conversation when I wondered wryly if karma was finally catching up to her, but I forced myself not to think that way. Being petty wasn't going to do me any good. Especially with that old familiar guilt gnawing at the back of my mind.

Because of it, I only really paid half of my attention to the meeting. Toby knew what was going on, so I let him approve of most of the decisions. I was certain if something truly abhorrent went up for debate and he was leaning toward it, my internal professional defense mechanisms would trigger, and I would be able to stop him. But that wasn't the most important thing on my mind.

My eyes wandered across the table and caught Jane's for a moment. She looked away quickly, but I kept watching her. I made the comparisons before, but now it was even more striking how different sweet Jane was from Angela. Being near my ex-wife again only exaggerated the stark differences between the two women. There were many bullet points I could go over to illustrate them, but the one standing out to me the most at that moment was how they responded to adversity and shifts in their lifestyle. Jane's parents cut her off and her response was to find a job and work hard for so much less than her trust fund would provide just to get by and have her own life. Angela got dumped by her rich husband and the next day she was on my doorstep, asking for help. It said so much about who they were as people.

It also put me in a strange position. A big part of me wanted to tell Angela to go lie in the bed she made and figure out life now that she knew what the man she chose over me was really like, but a bigger part of me didn't have that bitterness anymore. That was the response of a man still stinging from a divorce because of lingering feelings and wanting to hurt his ex because it made him feel good. That's not who I was and not the man I knew Jane would want me to be. I knew I had to do something, but as I sat there in the conference room partially paying attention to the meeting around me, I still didn't quite know what led my mind to the conclusion it did. I was still trying to process my way through the decision to offer her the penthouse suite of one of the hotels I owned.

Whatever led me to that moment, I did it and Angela readily and eagerly accepted. She left the office happy, but I couldn't say the same for me. Her happiness did nothing to take the painful tension out of Jane walking into the office. This wasn't the moment to reveal my relationship to Angela, and I didn't think it would be how Jane would want to go public, anyway. She deserved the chance to hear me tell her how I felt about her and agree to us being together. Yet, when I saw her face fall, I knew that wasn't the best way to handle it.

There wasn't anything I could do about that moment now. Now it was just about moving forward. I hoped Angela wouldn't be hanging around interfering in things for long. Maybe she would just take a few days away from everything and be able to move on.

I was still holding on to that hope the next morning. Angela didn't call me or try to get in touch with me at all after leaving the office. The hotel called me to confirm I sent her, and I assured them she was there as my guest, but that was the last I heard of it. And it was exactly my preference in the situation, so I wasn't going to press it.

That morning the first thing on my schedule was a meeting with Jane and Maddie. We were making last-minute adjustments to the launch schedule so we could be ready to get the campaign up and running. I was more focused on that meeting than I was the day before, but my mind was still wandering to Jane rather than to anything Maddie was saying. She kept her eyes away from me, only glancing my way when she needed to say something directly. Otherwise, she communicated with Maddie or looked down at the tablet in front of her.

There was distance between us. A heaviness had taken the place of the warmth and magnetic pull between us. I needed to figure out a way to get her alone so we could talk. Even if it meant barricading us in her office and not unlocking the door until we got the conversation out. Before I had the chance to even come up with a reason I needed to meet with her separately from Maddie, the door to the conference room burst open. I could hear my receptionist shouting in the instant before Angela stormed in.

The second she was inside, Jane's back straightened and her jaw set. She stared down at her tablet, jamming her finger onto the screen like she was working, though I doubt she was actually doing anything productive.

"Angela, what the hell are you doing here? You can't just barge in whenever you want," I said, standing and taking a step toward my ex.

My intention was to lead her right back out of the room, but she stepped around me and crossed the room away from the door, forcing me to pay attention to her.

"We have to talk, Nik," she said.

"Not right now. Again, I'm working. You need to go back to the penthouse—"

"That's just the problem," she said, cutting me off with a wave of her hand.

"What do you mean?" I asked.

"That so-called hotel of yours is not up to standard. I'm sorry, but I simply can't stay there. The sheets are like sandpaper. The staff is woefully undertrained. I went shopping this morning and was expected to carry my bags to the elevator myself. The spa's menu of services is wholly unacceptable. I called the front desk and requested a private session in my room and was told the options for something like that are extremely limited," she ranted. "So, I've had my things sent to your house. I'll be staying there for the time being."

When Angela paused for a breath, Jane and Maddie took the opportunity to stand up.

"We're going to step out," Maddie said. "Jane and I will continue what we can do between us."

I wanted to say something to stop them, but Angela stood with one hip cocked, staring them down like they were feeding right into what she wanted. They gathered their things and scurried out of the office, closing the door behind them. As soon as the door closed, I whipped around to face Angela.

"What do you think you're doing?" I demanded.

Angela instantly changed. The cold arrogance disappeared, and desperation filled her eyes. She dropped her face into her hands, and her shoulders shook as she cried. I walked over to her and took her by her upper arms to sit her down in one of the chairs around the conference table.

"I'm sorry," she said. "I shouldn't have come here this morning."

"What's going on?" I asked. "Why did you come to me at all? The truth, Angela. We've been divorced a damn decade."

"The truth? The truth is I really don't want to be alone, and you're all I have. It's a pretty sad reality that my ex-husband, who I haven't even had a conversation with in the last decade, is the only one I can turn to, but that's the truth. And..."

She looked down at her lap, her fingers twisting and pulling at each other.

"And, what?" I asked.

"I'm sick," she said.

And just like that, everything changed.

This was exactly what I worried about what we were in Paris. Despite the incredible connection between us and all we'd experienced together, we were going to get home and Nik would forget about all of it. Everything he said and all the beautiful ways he tried to make me feel special would disappear when we got back into the reality of New York and the pressure of the office. Worrying about it didn't take away the sting now that it was unfolding. I should have stuck to the plan I had originally. After confirming it with Elly, I should have just stayed with my first instinct and insisted we pretend nothing happened between us. Then, we might have had a chance of normalcy. If I did it, then there was a possibility I could put it behind me, and it wouldn't hurt so much. I'd asked for him to not think about it and for us to go on like there was nothing between us, but now that Nik was doing exactly that, it felt like the life had been sucked out of me.

A few weeks had gone by since getting back from Paris and having the unfortunate meeting with Angela. Nik was keeping his distance, not making any effort to pay me special attention or try to pick up the conversation where we'd left it off in Paris. He wasn't completely ignoring me. Somehow, that might have made it worse. If he was totally ignoring me, just acting like I wasn't there or doing his best to skirt around me when we were having meetings, it would let me be angry. Or at least miffed. Being ignored would seem active and purposeful. This just felt like he didn't care.

Continuing to work on the campaign while he kept his distance and interacted with me like I was just another of the team made me think of another very famous campaign that seemed to apply here. Only in my situation it was "What happened in Paris, stays in Paris." Maybe it was just the magic of the city that got into his mind and made him romantic and poetic. But once back in New York the sparkle faded, and it proved his talk was just talk. His distance coupled with his ex-wife now living in his house with him, not to mention showing up at the office all the time, I just assumed Nik lost interest.

"It just happened so fast," I said to Elly during what was becoming our once-monthly lunch date. "Less than forty-eight hours before she showed up, he called and asked me to go to dinner. The morning she reappeared was same morning he sent me flowers. How does a man go from sending a woman flowers to wanting nothing to do with her in less than a day?"

"Maybe it's all for the best," Elly told me. "You can go back to being a professional and not have to worry about an inappropriate relationship with your boss. Besides, Devin told me what that woman did to Nik. If he's really willing to take her back after all that, maybe he isn't the guy you thought he was."

I nodded and my stomach suddenly turned. I jumped to my feet and rushed to the bathroom. Elly came in after me, catching me just as I finished emptying my stomach in one of the stalls. She stood and waited until I emerged and went to the sink to rinse my face and mouth.

"Sorry," I said.

"Are you all right?" she asked. "That seemed to hit you fast."

"I just got suddenly nauseated. It's been happening a lot recently," I told her.

"What do you mean?"

"I've been throwing up after lunch all week. I think the stress of this whole stupid situation is just getting to me," I explained. Elly didn't respond and I looked into the mirror at her reflection. She stared back at me with widened eyes. "What?"

"You've been throwing up after lunch all week?" she asked.

"Yes."

"Jane, when was your last period?" Elly asked.

My mouth fell open as the realization rushed over me. The possibility hadn't even occurred to me. It was far from my mind, not something I was even thinking about. But it had popped right into Elly's head, and she wasn't afraid to point it out. Could I be pregnant?

"Oh, God," I said. "You don't think...? Come on. We need to get to the drugstore right now."

We paid for our partially eaten lunch and rushed to the nearest drugstore. I stood in front of the display of pregnancy tests feeling like I was reading a different language. I had no idea which one to pick. Elly stepped up beside me and snagged one from the display.

"This one," she said. "I got a really clear result, super-fast with this one."

"Was it right?" I asked.

She stared at me incredulously and looked down at her rounded belly, then back at me.

"Yes. It was right."

I nodded. "Okay."

We bought three of the same tests, but I didn't have the patience to wait until after work to take the test at my apartment. There was no way I was going to bring it back to the office with me and take it there. Instead, Elly and I hurried into the drugstore bathroom. I took all three tests and lined them up on the edge of the sink to wait. Those three minutes took an eternity to pass by. When they finally did, I looked down at the tests and felt my knees buckle.

Leaning back against the wall, I slid down to the floor, not even processing or caring that I was in a public bathroom. Elly came up beside me and crouched down to wrap her arms around me comfortingly.

"All three of them are positive," I confirmed.

She held me tighter and nodded.

"We'll figure something out," she said.

I shook my head. "What is there to figure out? I'm pregnant. I'm carrying my boss's child. A boss who is now back with his ex-wife, I might add."

"When are you going to tell him?" Elly asked.

I stared at her for a second, sure she had to be joking, then shook my head hard again.

"Oh, no. I'm not telling him. At least not right now. I'm keeping quiet about this," I told her.

Elly looked concerned. "Jane, you know that wasn't such a great strategy when I did it."

"This is different, Elly. I just can't say anything right now. I just can't."

Elly and I parted ways, and as much as I wanted to go home and wallow, I went back to the office. Everyone, including Nik, would notice if I just didn't come back and would try to figure out what was going on. I needed to act like everything was normal so no one would suspect anything.

I managed not to give anything away, and it seemed like I'd skate through the day when I got a call that afternoon.

"Hello?" I said.

"Jane, it's Preston," the voice said through the line.

I rolled my eyes. Of course it was. Because I needed a few more things to be stressed about in that moment.

"What do you want, Preston? I'm at work," I said.

"I know. I won't keep you. I just wanted to ask if you'll join me for dinner tonight," he invited.

"Dinner?" I asked, the hesitation obvious in my voice.

"Yes. Dinner," he said.

"There's no point, Preston. There's nothing for us to talk about."

"But there is, Jane. I have a proposition for you. A business pitch if you will," he said.

I thought about my options and the news that was still trying to sink in. Finally, I relented. It wasn't like I was going to be able to keep my job with the marketing team for much longer. I was going to need to resign soon enough before Nik had the chance to notice my pregnancy. Maybe Preston wouldn't be wasting my time.

"All right, Preston. I will meet you for dinner. Just tell me when and where," I agreed.

THAT EVENING I arrived at the restaurant slightly late. That seemed to be an ongoing theme with me that day. The host led me across the dining floor to a table where Preston already sat with a glass of wine. I sat down and tried to offer him a smile, but it probably came across as more like a grimace.

"Hello, Preston," I said congenially.

"Hello, Jane," he replied.

The waiter came by with a second glass and reached to pick up the bottle of wine Preston had ordered. I shook my hands in front of the glass to stop him.

"No, thank you," I said.

Preston looked at me questioningly. "No wine?"

"No. I've had quite enough wine recently," I told him. "So, Preston, why are we here?"

"You get straight to it, don't you?"

"I see no purpose in doing things any other way," I said.

"All right," he said, leaning slightly toward me. "I know you've been getting a lot of flak from your parents about our potential marriage, and now my parents have started to up the pressure, too. Look, I don't want to marry you either, but at least you're not so bad."

"Um... thanks?"

"No, I'm serious, Jane. I can't give up my lifestyle as easily as you seem to be able to. I can't see either set of parents backing down anytime soon. Which means we need a creative solution," he told me.

"What did you have in mind?" I asked.

"We get married—but in name only. We can both do whatever we want, date whoever we want, as long as it stays discreet. We can go about our own separate lives like we always have, just possibly been seen together a couple of times here and there. We'll stay together long enough for us to divorce amicably. Then we go our separate ways having satisfied our parents and secured our financial holdings," he said.

I was temporarily stunned. It really did seem like the answer to all my problems. If I went through with this, I wouldn't have to worry about losing my job with the marketing team. I would have enough money to raise the baby and continue building a life for myself. For us. And if Preston wasn't interested in a sexual relationship with me, just as I was clearly not interested in one with him, then maybe it wouldn't be anywhere near as bad as I dreaded.

I couldn't believe it. I was actually about to tell Preston we might as well try it, but out of the corner of my eye, I noticed something that took the words out of my mouth. Nik sat at a table on the far end of the dining room with several other men wearing suits.

CHAPTER 21

NIK

Business dinners were not among my favorite things about running my company. Depending on the people I was meeting with, they could be fun. The majority of the time, though, I dreaded sitting at the table with a bunch of stuffed suits sifting through negotiations and dry conversation. That was the kind I was dealing with that night. The men were doing their best to posture, peacocking to make themselves seem far more powerful and important than they actually were. I encountered that often during meetings like this. People puffing themselves up and trying to impress or even intimidate me into making better deals with them. It never failed to cool me to working with them.

A particularly self-congratulatory ramble about his accomplishments had my mind wandering away from the meeting, and I started looking around the restaurant. My eyes fell on a table across the room, locking on Jane staring back at me. I didn't want to believe I was seeing her there. It had been a few weeks since we'd had any time together, but that didn't make it any easier to see her sitting at the table with another man. The guy sitting across from her was handsome and around her age. His lean toward her made me go rigid and everything around me fade out. I didn't care about anything the men were saying or anything else happening. I wasn't just going to sit by and let Jane have a date right in front of me without making myself known. Even if I had absolutely no right to be upset given my recent behavior.

"Excuse me one second, gentlemen. I see an associate I need to speak with. Continue enjoying your dinner. I'll be right back," I said.

The man speaking started to protest, getting red-faced at the thought of me leaving the table right in the middle of his autobiography, but I didn't care. I stood and buttoned my suit jacket as I made my way across the restaurant toward Jane. She watched me approach, occasionally flitting her eyes back to the man across from her.

"Jane, what a surprise," I said when I got to the edge of the table. "It's nice running into you."

"Hello," she said. I looked pointedly at the man across from her, then back at her. Finally, she held out a hand toward him. "This is Nik Nygard, my boss. Nik, this is Preston Howell."

I instantly went on the defensive. I knew that name. She'd said it to me when we were in Paris and she explained why the landlady was so excited to have her back in the apartment. This was the guy her parents wanted her to marry, and she'd refused so vehemently she was willing to accept being cut off. And yet here she was, having dinner with him. What the fuck was going on?

Jane could see the tension in my expression. I could tell by the way she looked back at me. But she didn't say anything. There was no explanation, no reassurance. She just picked up her glass of water and took a sip as she seemed to wait for me to walk away. That wasn't going to happen. I took a step closer to her.

"Jane, I'd like to have a moment of your time," I said.

She made no move to get up. Instead, she set her glass down and tilted her head at me.

"I'm sorry. I'm having dinner with Preston right now," she said. "Whatever it is can wait until morning I'm sure."

"It's important," I said, trying to keep the frustration out of my voice. "I need to speak with you about something work-related."

"I'm not at work right now. We can schedule a time to talk tomorrow morning," she repeated.

"It was nice meeting you," Preston said in the flat, emotionless way people born wealthy are taught to do by the time they learn to speak. He was clearly trying to dismiss me and I wasn't having it.

"Excuse us a minute. You'll be able to get back to your dinner shortly. I just need to speak to Jane," I said.

Preston looked at Jane, who let out a deep sigh but still didn't make a move to join me. My frustration was turning to anger, and Jane could see it. She stared directly at me; her expression impossible to read.

"You can't just knock the guy out of his chair this time," she said. "It doesn't work that way." She turned to Preston. "Give me just a second. I'm sorry about this."

"Are you finished?" Preston asked, glancing at her plate. "Do you want dessert?"

Jane shook her head. "I'm finished. Thank you. Go ahead and pay the check and call your driver. I won't be long."

Preston nodded and got up from the table. He walked toward the front of the restaurant, and I immediately slid into his chair. I leaned toward Jane so I could talk to her without everyone around us hearing me.

"What are you doing?" I asked.

She glanced around casually like she didn't understand what I was asking.

"I'm having dinner with a friend," she answered. "At least, I was until my boss showed up and started acting crazy."

"A friend? Preston Howell is not your friend. That's the man your delusional parents tried to pawn you off on in exchange for a goat and some silk or some shit like that. You wanted nothing to do with him the last time I heard. So don't pull that," I said, my voice coming out as a harsh half-whisper.

I didn't mean to sound so aggressive, but the anger bubbling up inside me was undeniable. She glared at me, emotion finally showing up on her face. But it definitely wasn't the emotion I wanted. She didn't look happy to see me or even embarrassed to have been caught having dinner with Preston. She looked furious.

"What the hell do you care? The last time I checked, you were back shacking up with your ex-wife," she shot at me. She didn't give me time to reply before she stood up sharply and dropped her napkin to the table. "I'm tired, Nik, and since you don't really have an urgent work issue to discuss with me, I'm leaving."

She started to walk away, and I stood, reaching out to grab her arm so she couldn't get past me.

"We need to talk, Jane," I said.

She yanked her arm away and continued past, walking out of the restaurant.

I rushed after her, forgetting about the men waiting for me at the table. They didn't have much of a chance at landing a deal with me, anyway. This was just going to save them the humiliation of my rejection. As I burst out of the restaurant, I saw Jane walk up to Preston. He reached out to take her by her upper arms, and I closed the space between us in three long strides.

"Let your driver know there will only be one stop tonight. I'll be taking Jane home. We need to talk," I told Preston in no uncertain terms.

Preston looked at Jane.

"Is that all right with you, Jane?" he asked.

Jane finally shrugged. Clearly, she finally realized I was not in the mood to be trifled with and the night would go more smoothly for everyone if she just stopped resisting me.

"Go ahead," she said.

"Call me if you need anything," he told her.

"I promise you'll hear from me soon," she answered.

A white car pulled up to the front of the restaurant, and Preston climbed into the back seat. Jane let me lead her to my waiting SUV, and I opened the back door, gesturing for her to get inside. I followed her in and shut the door behind us. My driver started toward her apartment, and I pressed the button to close the privacy shield between the front and back of the car.

"All right, Nik. Now you've gotten me here. What is it you want to talk about?" she asked.

"You can do better than resort to marrying that loser," I told her.

"That's not really any of your business," she retorted.

"It is absolutely my business," I disagreed.

"How do you figure that?" she asked, her voice raising slightly. "You haven't said more than a couple of words to me in weeks. You've barely even acknowledged my existence outside of meetings, and even then, it's only business. Why should you feel like you have any say at all in what I decide to do with my life?"

"It's been a difficult time for me," I told her.

I started to say more, but Jane held up her hand to stop me.

"There's really no need for you to explain," she said. "I have eyes in my head."

"What's that supposed to mean?" I demanded.

At that moment the car pulled up to the curb in front of her apartment building, and Jane jumped out without answering. I took off my seat belt and scrambled out of the car after her. I pursued her all the way up the stairs until we stopped at her door. She whipped around to face me.

"Chasing me all the way up here is pointless. We have nothing to talk about," she announced.

"I'm not leaving until you tell me if you've changed your mind and are marrying that prick," I said through gritted teeth.

Jane's shoulders dropped, and she let out a breath.

"Go away, Nik," she said, opening the door just enough for her to slip inside.

I pushed my way into the door and slammed it closed behind me.

"I want an answer," I said forcefully.

She didn't look thrown off by my tone or at all flustered by me following her. She looked tired. She shook her head.

"You shouldn't care," she said. "You've got your own wife to worry about."

"Ex-wife," I shouted.

She walked around me and opened the door, then flattened her hands on my chest, trying to shove me out of the apartment.

"Frankly, Nik, I don't care how many ways you try to modify it. You still have her living in your house and have been ignoring me since we got back from Paris," she said.

Grabbing her by her shoulders, I spun her around and pushed her up against the door, closing it at the same time I crushed my mouth over hers to silence her. She resisted at first, trying to push me away, but when I pulled away from the kiss, she stared at me with a fire burning in her eyes. I came down on her again, kissing her passionately and pressing my body against hers. Jane struggled again, but a second later, her arms looped around my neck and her mouth opened against mine. She kissed me back just as intensely, groaning as I bit down into her bottom lip.

Without saying a word, I grabbed her up into my arms and carried her a few steps farther into the living room to the couch. Tipping her backward onto the cushions, I came down on top of her and kissed her harder. I couldn't slow down. I didn't want to. Anger and frustration continued to surge through me, and the only thing that kept it down was touching her. It was a possessive, consuming rage. Jane was mine. Not Preston's, not anyone's. She belonged to me, and there was nothing that was going to change that.

The dress she'd worn to dinner was easy to push up to her waist, and I tore her shoes away from her feet. Not bothering to take off my belt, I pulled down my zipper and took out my already hard cock. She wore pale lavender satin panties that night, and they easily pulled to the side so I could plunge inside her. Jane let out a sound somewhere between a growl and a scream and arched her back. I slammed into her, not even slowing down to take a breath.

CHAPTER 22

JANE

I reached between Nik and me to claw at the buckle of his belt. It finally opened and I pushed it away before releasing the button on his pants. Nik pulled out of me long enough to push his pants and boxers down his legs while I tugged my panties away. It only took a few seconds, but it was enough to leave me feeling empty and aching for Nik to be inside me again. I was fumbling with the buttons on his shirt when he pushed forward again, and the intensity of my body stretching to hold him so quickly made my hands fall away.

Nik's mouth was hungry on mine. It was less a kiss than a claim, possessing me. I responded in kind, taking his tongue into my mouth and clawing at his back. Hot tears stung in my eyes, and my heart felt like it was tearing in two. The emotion of what was going on between us overwhelmed me. Part of me was so angry, so filled with disappointment and a sense of rejection and abandonment. I wanted to push Nik away, to scream at him and tell him exactly the pain he was putting me through. I wanted to tell him I was going to marry Preston, just to watch the hurt on his face and know I was giving him even a fraction of what he did to me.

The other part of me clung desperately to him. I missed him so much. It felt like part of me was missing being away from him. Every second we were apart it got worse. Every day in the office when I couldn't just reach out and touch him, or steal a kiss, chipped away at me. I needed him in a way I never experienced and wanted to hold him close to me, never letting him go.

We battled each other with our bodies. Every kiss, bite, and deep thrust said what we couldn't put into words. We were combustible. Any moment we could burst into flames and fully consume each other. I gave myself over to it willingly. I needed this more than anything, even as I knew it was the last thing I should be doing.

My orgasm hit me without warning, and I screamed out with the intensity of it tearing through my body. An instant later, Nik let out a primal roar and I felt him spilling into me, his body shuddering as he wrapped his arms around me. We clung to each other, suspended in that moment. My vision blurred, and I couldn't hear anything but the rush of blood in my ears and Nik gasping for breath. Squeezing my eyes closed, I let the tears slide down my cheeks and soak into his shirt. I didn't want him to move or speak. The second he did, this would all be real, and I would have to acknowledge it. I kept my arms around him, and my head buried in the side of his neck until my body relaxed and reality rushed back.

I didn't know how to feel. Nik stretched out on the couch with me, his head rested beside mine and our legs intertwined, but it felt like we were a million miles apart. I couldn't get my emotions straight or even know what to think. If he really was back with his ex-wife, this was incredibly wrong. That would mean I was just a party to cheating, and I couldn't abide that. There were many choices I'd made in my life, and some of them I wasn't completely proud of, but I wouldn't be someone's mistress.

Moving out from under him, I adjusted my dress and smoothed my hair.

"You need to leave," I told Nik without looking at him.

"Jane," he started, pulling himself up to sit.

"I need you to go, now," I said firmly.

He adjusted his clothes, getting dressed again, but didn't get up to leave. I wiped away the tears as he slid closer to me. He was suddenly tender, lightly stroking my back as he leaned closer to speak softly to me.

"Jane, please. We need to talk. We need to have a serious conversation about what's going on," he said.

I couldn't look at him. It hurt too much to even think about looking into his eyes. Instead, I shook my head.

"I need space, Nik. I need time to think," I told him.

"No, Jane. You don't need time to think about this. You can't marry Preston Howell. Remember what it was like for you when your parents first told you that's what they wanted you to do. Remember how angry you were and that you were willing to walk away from everything to stop it from happening. Think about us in Paris."

Suddenly, it was all too much for me. Nik was trying to hold on to me while simultaneously keeping his ex-wife. He wanted it all. Me not having my parents' status and money anymore meant I wasn't a good enough match for a society partner. He wanted the beautiful, sophisticated, cultured wife he could bring to events, while keeping me on the side for his amusement. He wanted both, and that wasn't an option. It would never work. Not from me.

That didn't even take into account my pregnancy. He still had no idea I was carrying his child. There were several times already when I wanted to tell him. I could have just blurted it out when we were in the back of his SUV or when he first came into the apartment. I could have told him before he carried me to the couch or stopped him and told him when we were tearing away each other's clothes. But every time I started to let it out, I couldn't get the words to come. When I got close, I remembered Nik was going home to Angela and it stopped me. I couldn't bring myself to tell him, knowing it would be just a way to manipulate his emotions. If he was going to choose me, he would have. I wanted him to want me, not to have an obligation.

"Nik, you need to leave," I said again. "Right now."

"Jane..."

"Now."

It tore me to pieces, but I kept myself together as he nodded and got to his feet. He finished adjusting his clothes and started to the door. I followed behind him and stopped when he turned around to look at me. He started to say something but stopped himself and walked out of the apartment. I locked the door behind him and pressed my back to it, gasping for breath through the pain in my chest. Sliding down to sit on the floor, I wrapped my arms around my knees and let myself cry. These were far from the first tears I'd cried for Nik, and I was sure they weren't going to be the last. There was no point in fighting the emotion. It was my reality. I had to live with it now.

When I cried all the tears my body could make, I dragged myself up off the floor and went to the tiny bathroom to take a shower. As I stood there under the water that was never hot enough and never had enough pressure behind it, I decided I couldn't take it anymore. I couldn't bear it. I had to get out of there. I had to get out of my job, out of my cramped apartment. Just out of New York City altogether. I dropped into bed and fell asleep with wet hair and a heavy heart.

The next morning, I woke up feeling calm. It wasn't a happy or content calm. Just a sense of resolve and the steadiness that came with knowing what was ahead of me. I made myself a cup of coffee, looked out the window at daybreak over the horizon, and called Preston.

"Hello?"

His voice was groggy. I'd obviously woken him, but I didn't care. He needed to hear this, and if I didn't say it now, I might push it away again.

"Yes," I said.

"What?" he asked.

"I agree to the engagement."

"Jane is that you?" he asked, sounding slightly more awake now.

"Do you have multiple women you are juggling potential engagements with?" I asked.

It wasn't that outlandish a question. I'd known more than one man who thought keeping his options open meant proposing to several women and deciding which to keep over the course of several weeks. It was like a queasy, far less romantic version of *The Bachelor*.

"No," Preston confirmed.

"Good. Then it's just me. I agree to the engagement."

"Really?"

"Yes. After talking to you last night, I realized it really is what's in both of our best interests. Like you said, it will be a marriage in name only. We will leverage the power of both families and create a mutually beneficial arrangement to appease our parents. And when an appropriate length of time has passed, we can divorce quietly and continue on as friends. It is really what's best for everyone," I told him.

"That's wonderful," Preston said. "Should we make a formal announcement?"

"Not yet. Let's just tell our parents, and we'll go from there."

He agreed and we got off the phone to individually call our parents. Mine responded exactly the way I thought they would, lavishing me with praise and excitement just as if I'd told them I was deliriously in love and thrilled to get married. It was insincere. I didn't genuinely think it was best for either of us, or even that it was a great decision, but saying I did unlocked my bank account and delivered me right back into the life I'd left behind. It was what I needed. Agreeing to the arrangement bought me some time and provided me the space I needed to think and figure out what to do next. Maybe I would still call everything off. I might still decide to just do this all on my own. Right now, I needed the breathing room.

As soon as I got off the phone with my parents, I went into action. Now that I was rich again, I sent an email of resignation to Maddie, then went into my bedroom and packed my bags. One week of working in Paris wasn't enough. I needed to lose myself in my favorite city and try to find out what life meant now.

That night I sat on the long flight to France, staring out the window at the darkness beyond. I tucked my head against my pillow and pulled a blanket up over me, then let my eyes drift closed. Almost immediately, I fell asleep and faded away into a blissful dream.

Nik took me by my hands and guided me into the moonlight spread like liquid silver across the wooden floor. The evening air came through the large open windows over-

looking Paris and fluttered the thin gauzy nightgown I wore. He lifted his hand to twirl me around and brought me into his arms. His shirtless chest and taut abs felt hot against me, and I melted into the clean, spicy scent of him. We danced slowly in the shimmering light. Nik touched a kiss to the side of my neck, and I closed my eyes, sighing at the brush of his lips.

I ran my hands up his strong, muscled arms and down his chest. My fingertips traced the ripple of his abs and swept along his waistband, dipping down just enough to touch skin hidden by his pants. Every movement was slow and gentle, unrushed as if we had all the time in the world together. I could hear soft strains of music around us, and they became like our own breaths and the touch of our kiss as our bodies moved closer. Nik slipped his fingers beneath the straps of my nightgown and eased them down my shoulders, tenderly guiding them out of the way until the gown fell out of place and pooled at my feet. I wore nothing beneath it, and he brushed his hands over the peaks of my breasts as he gazed at me.

He made me feel beautiful, cherished, and exquisite. I wanted nothing more than the touch of his hands and the taste of his lips.

CHAPTER 23

NIK

Jane's skin was soft and sweet under my lips. I indulged myself with a long sweep of my tongue across her collarbone, then paused at the soft spot at the base of her throat. Touching my lips there, I could feel the trembling rhythm of her heartbeat beneath the skin. Her fingers combed through my hair, and she leaned down to kiss my head. Lowering down to my knees, I rested my head against her stomach, wrapping my arms around her waist to cradle her close. My hands ran down the back of her legs and carefully eased them apart. She moaned as I dipped my head forward to taste her and slid my fingers inside.

I loved the sound of that moan. It filled my heart and woke up my body. Every time I heard those sounds slip out of her, I needed her more. It took every bit of control I had to not just plunge inside her. That would make it end too fast. I needed more of her than that. I took a few moments to worship her, to show my reverence to her gorgeous body, before taking my fingers from her and sitting back so I could draw her down into my lap. Sitting on the floor, I held Jane by her hips to hold her steady as I sank into her and cradled her in my arms.

She rolled her body, rocking her hips to grind into my lap and sliding her breasts against my chest. Her hands on my shoulders gave her leverage, and I watched her with awe and pleasure. She was uninhibited, unafraid of seeking after everything she wanted. She knew what her body needed and how to use mine to get it. I was more than happy to give it to her and felt myself losing control as I watched her breasts bounce and sweat drip along her skin. She leaned back and propped herself up on her hands, moving her feet so they were propped on the floor on either side of my hips. The new position opened her legs so she was on display for me. I reached between us to swirl my thumb over her clit.

Hot and wet, her body accepted my touch eagerly, and she bucked her hips against my hand. The pleasure built up inside me, climbing up my legs and into my stomach. I lifted my hips to thrust up into her harder and faster. I reached to grab her head and pull it to me for a deep kiss, but just as our mouths crashed together, my eyes snapped open.

Jane wasn't there. I was alone in my bed, sweating and gripping the sheets beside me. My head was pounding, and I immediately felt angry and unfulfilled. I buried my head in the pillow and let out a growl. The sun wasn't even up yet, so I pulled the blankets up and tried to force myself back to sleep. Maybe I'd be able to find Jane again and find the fulfillment I needed. But I couldn't sleep. My mind was racing too fast. After another twenty minutes of tossing around in the bed, I gave up and dragged myself into the bathroom to take a shower. I turned the heat of the water up until it stung on my skin, the massage setting at its most intense. Standing with my head hanging, I let the stream pound into my muscles.

By the time I got into the kitchen, I still wasn't feeling any better. I was having a seriously shitty morning. I hated the way things had gone with Jane the night before. That wasn't anything like I envisioned for the next time we had a chance to be alone together. I wanted to hold her in my arms and tell her everything I was feeling, then spend the night making love to her. It didn't go that way. I didn't even get a chance to explain about Angela and why she was at my house. Seeing her sitting at that table with Preston made my brain go out the window, and I acted on instinct alone.

Holding my tongue for the last few weeks had been a mistake. I thought keeping my distance and not pushing her after she saw Angela and me together would give Jane the time to think and let things settle in. Now I knew I should have talked to her about everything. I should have approached her and made her understand.

But I had no idea how long this Angela situation was going to last. If I'd known, I never would have waited to get to Jane. I wanted to protect her from the mistakes of my past so she wouldn't be dragged into thinking I might repeat them. In doing that, I managed to fuck it up anyway. Jane threw me out of her apartment with barely a word and hadn't answered the phone when I'd called her. This had to end here. I couldn't let it keep going. I had to come clean with Jane right away.

I reached into the refrigerator for orange juice and was halfway through pouring a glass when Angela stomped into the kitchen. The glare on her face was enough to tell me she wasn't there to brighten my day with the announcement she was moving out, effectively immediately. I reminded myself why I let her stay with me to begin with and shoved the juice back in the refrigerator.

"How do you expect me to live like this, Nik?" she demanded.

"What's wrong now, Angela?" I asked.

"You don't even have a cook. How is that possible?" she demanded.

"I haven't had a cook for as long as you've been here. You seem to be doing just fine," I pointed out.

"I've had to scavenge for food. That isn't the way it should be for someone in my condition."

Her voice had slipped into the simpering tone she used to manipulate people into doing what she wanted. It didn't work on me. It never had.

"If you are concerned about your health, Angela, maybe this isn't the place for you. I don't have a cook, and I'm not going to hire one. It's never been necessary before, and it's not necessary now," I told her.

"Julius had a chef at each of his estates who was on call twenty-four hours a day. Anything I needed or wanted, he made for me. That's what I'm accustomed to," she said.

There was a hint in her voice, something that said she was trying to make me compete with her soon-to-be ex. I had enough shit going on in my head to not add her petty complaints to it, too.

"Like I said, I have no need for an on-call chef. I can take care of myself just fine," I said.

"I disagree. You might not have a problem with mediocre meals, but I can't keep calling out for food all the time," she argued.

"Why don't you try going to the grocery store and cooking some actual meals for a change?"

Angela glared at me like I'd grown another head and it was spewing out blasphemy. Her hand pressed her heart, and if she wasn't born and raised in New York, I would have sworn she was going to pull a *Gone with the Wind* and gotten the vapors.

"I don't appreciate being treated this callously when I came to you for help," she said in an affected, gasping voice.

I downed the rest of my juice and put the glass in the dishwasher.

"You haven't been appreciative of any of the help I've been giving you, which is quite a bit," I pointed out.

The pouting look left her face, and Angela smiled, lowering her eyelashes and coming toward me with a slow, wiggling walk. She slipped her arms around my neck, and before I realized what was happening, she leaned in and kissed me. I pushed her back and moved away from her.

"What are you doing?" I asked.

She laughed and came toward me.

"I'm showing you my appreciation," she said, lunging toward me for another kiss.

Catching her by her wrists, I moved her back away from me.

"That's not what I meant, Angela."

She shrugged casually and leaned against the counter. "I've decided to give you another chance."

She said it matter-of-factly, like it was a foregone conclusion I would readily accept it.

"You're what?" I asked incredulously.

"Giving you another chance. I made a mistake ten years ago, but we can make up for lost time now," she said.

She said the words seductively, but I was far from it having any effect.

"I am not interested in making up for any lost time. That ship has sailed," I told her.

She blinked a few times. "What are you talking about, Nik?"

"I don't want to be with you. I have feelings for someone else."

She closed the space between us and pressed her body against mine.

"Come on, Nik. You don't mean that. This is me. Remember how good it was between us? Remember how happy we were?"

I took her arms and set her away from me again.

"Look, I'm sorry. I know this is a bad time for us to be having this conversation considering your health, but I need to be clear with you."

She started giggling and shook her head. "Is that what you're worried about? I have a little secret for you." She leaned closer and dropped her voice to a whisper. "I'm not sick."

"What?" I demanded, my stomach dropping.

She shook her head again. "I'm not sick." My jaw set and she gave a bratty sigh. "Well, what did you expect me to do? You didn't want to pay any attention to me and were just going to send me away. I needed you, and even you are too good of a guy to send away someone who might be dying. I knew once we spent some time together again you would see we should be back together. Then I would be miraculously healed, and we could live happily ever after."

The smile on her pink-painted lips made me want to either throw up or smash something.

"What the fuck is wrong with you?" I asked.

Her face dropped.

"What's wrong, Nikky?" she simpered.

"Don't you even fucking try that. You lied to me about having a life-threatening illness so you could move into my house? You seriously thought you could just come here and

I was going to... what? Fall so desperately in love with you I wouldn't care that you're a lying psychopath?"

"It isn't like that," she started. "I was just—"

"Pack your shit and get out," I commanded.

Her eyes widened. "What?"

"I said pack your shit and get out," I repeated, lowering my voice and slowing my words to ensure she understood every single syllable.

"You can't be serious," she said, all the lightness out of her voice.

"Pack or I'll have my driver do it. I don't give a shit what happens to any of it. When I get home, you better be gone."

I didn't stay in the kitchen long enough for her to respond. Storming out of the house, I called my driver and headed for work. I was still fuming when I got into the office, but my strides were long and resolute. I had a mission ahead of me. Jane wasn't going to buck me so easily this time. She was going to listen to what I had to say to her, and we were going to get this straightened out between us. I needed her more than ever, and I wasn't going to let her slip through my fingers.

I stalked to the marketing department and right to her office. But it was dark, the door shut. Thinking she might have gone straight to Maddie's office to keep working on the campaign, I headed there. Maddie looked up from her desk when I walked into the office.

"Good morning, Nik," she said before the expression on my face registered. "Oh. You must have heard."

"Heard what?" I asked.

"Jane resigned."

"Yes, Mother, Preston and I are still getting married. I'm just taking some time to enjoy my last months of freedom," I said over the phone, trying hard not to roll my eyes. "Of course, plans are coming along. You have nothing to worry about," I reassured her before hanging up.

Of course, it was a total lie, considering still no one knew that I was carrying another man's child.

I had only meant to visit Paris for a few weeks. Spending time there with the marketing team had been wonderful, and the lure of my favorite city was too strong to resist when I was at such a low point. It felt like my life had been thrown up into the air and I was just waiting for the pieces of it to fall back to earth. So until that happened, I wanted to be somewhere I loved, enjoying a few weeks until I had to face whatever as going to happen next.

Once I got there, I knew it wasn't going to be that simple. The city was a bubble, protecting me from reality back in New York. What had started as a plan to only be there for a few weeks turned into a month, then another, and another. Staying in the same rental reclaimed it from the team and made it mine again. Just like it had been before I'd ever brought them there, it was the setting of my favorite memories and the place where I was comfortable and happy. Not that it went completely smoothly. Being back there still required some getting used to.

For the first several weeks, I couldn't even look at the door that led to the bedroom where Nik had stayed. I purposely chose a different bedroom, so I wasn't so close to the one where he'd slept. After a while, I was used to it enough to walk past the door without averting my eyes. Finally, I came to terms with it. Since then, I existed alongside the specter of him there. I didn't acknowledge it, but it didn't plague me quite as much. It was like a more painful version of living with a burned-out lightbulb. It was there every day and I couldn't help but notice it, but it just became a part of my life.

Marguerite helped. The landlady was thrilled to have me back and teased she'd barely had a chance to get the place cleaned before I bounced back after leaving. Of course, that wasn't true. The apartment was pristine when I arrived back in it. Even though she had only a day's notice, it was freshly cleaned and filled with fresh flower arrangements. The dining table was laden with food and wine, and she arrived the next morning with a massive basket of croissants and coffee. It seemed like as good an opportunity as any to tell her about the baby. I handed her back the bottle of wine and demurred from drinking the coffee, but ate approximately half my weight in the rich, indescribably delicious croissants.

She was excited about the baby and left with the wine still sitting on the table. For the future, she told me. For a special occasion. She was doting on me even more since my pregnancy was really starting to show. My rounded belly seemed to call out to her, and barely a day went by she didn't show up with pastries, fruit, or bread and cheese. She spoke French to the baby and whispered wishes for its future like she was a self-appointed fairy godmother. It was endearing, and I greatly appreciated the company and support. The six months in Paris were spent alone. No one had come to visit, and even my family's attempts to lure me back had petered off within the first few weeks. They were just happy I'd agreed to marry Preston.

I was glad they didn't argue with my insistence on a long engagement. Not only did it release me from the immediate obligation of planning a fraudulent wedding, but it gave me time to think about how I was going to introduce them to their grandchild. I was going to have a lot to explain when I showed back up with a baby that wasn't Preston's. Not that it mattered. It didn't take long away from New York for me to decide I couldn't go through with the wedding after all. I wouldn't marry a man I didn't love, not even to secure a financial future for myself and my child.

Which left me with no options. My reality was the man I loved was back with his ex, and I was about to have a baby with no father. I ran my hand over my belly as I walked into the kitchen for an afternoon snack.

"What do you think, baby? What sounds good to you?"

Talking to the baby was my favorite part of the day. I loved it already, and I knew I would do everything in my power to be a good mother, no matter what. That didn't require anyone else. Taking care of my baby and making sure I gave it the best life possible was my top priority now and that didn't mean it was going to be easy. When it finally came time for me to stop hiding in Paris and go home, I'd have to figure out how to build that life for us. I knew I was going to have some tough choices to make, and it may not always go smoothly, but I could do it. Maddie would probably give me a good reference, which took some of the trepidation away from looking for another job. With a good word from her behind me, I could get a new position that would allow me to provide the best I could as a working single mother.

It was a daunting thought that came to mind yet again as I stood in front of the refrigerator. This happened more and more often the longer I was in Paris. Simple tasks suddenly seemed so much harder and made me think about how different my future was going to be. And more often than not, it ended the same way it did right then—with tears streaming down my face. Damn it. All I wanted was something to eat while I curled up on the couch with a good book, but the debate between a bowl of fruit and a slab of bread with butter ended with me leaning back against the counter, sobbing as reality sank in. Like it usually did, that made my mind drift to Nik. As much as I tried not to think about him, to keep my thoughts and emotions at bay and not dwell on what could have been, I couldn't stop myself.

I missed him more every day. It was getting more intense the more the baby grew. Every movement reminded me of what we were missing together. I loved the baby so much and was more excited by the minute to meet my child but knew Nik should be there experiencing it with me.

My phone ringing managed to snap me out of my crying, and I went into the living room to find it.

"Hey, Elly," I said, trying to draw in a breath and wiping my tears off my cheeks.

"Are you all right?" she asked.

I nodded even though she couldn't see me and dropped down onto the couch.

"Yes," I told her.

"Are you lying?"

"Yes."

"What's going on?" she asked.

"I was trying to pick a snack," I told her.

"You're crying because you couldn't figure out what you wanted for a snack?" she asked.

"No," I told her. "Well, yes. But no. I was just standing there in the kitchen, looking into the refrigerator, and all I could think about was that I shouldn't be getting my own snack. Then you know what I realized? I am going to be getting my own snacks for the rest of my life. Whenever I need something to eat, I'm going to have to get it for myself."

Elly made a sound like she was trying to figure out what to say.

"Haven't you been making your own snacks for a while?" she asked.

"It's not the snacks, Elly. I know how ridiculous and petty that sounds. It's everything. It's my whole future. I was standing there in the kitchen thinking about having a snack, and it sank in I'm not going to just be able to hide out in Paris forever. Eventually, I'm going to have to face reality. The baby is coming soon, and I'm going to have to go back to the States and break the news to my family and Preston. Which, of course, will mean I won't have any money anymore, and I'm going to have to get a job and figure out my life," I told her.

"Well, you might not want to delay that too much," she said.

"Are you seriously pressuring me to find a job right now?" I let out a sigh. "Fine. Do you have any more leads for me? I went right to the top with the last one."

I leaned forward and rested my head in my hand, massaging my suddenly aching temples.

"That's not what I meant, actually. I'm guessing you don't do much in the way of reading American newspapers over there in Paris? The *Times* in particular?" she asked.

It was such an odd question it made me lift my head up. That was the type of question people in terrible TV movies ask when they are standing on the other side of the door waiting to surprise their long-lost friend. But considering Elly had a new baby of her own, I highly doubted that was what was happening.

"What are you talking about?" I asked.

"You made an appearance in the newspaper this morning," she told me.

"Did Preston report me missing?" I asked, only partially kidding.

We'd only spoken on the phone twice since I'd come to Paris, and he was less than pleased at my insistence at staying here. As much as they said they understood us wanting a long engagement and supported us, a complete lack of wedding planning wasn't sitting well with our parents. According to him, for our plan to continue working they wanted us to make a few appearances in public. We knew the rules of society. An engagement didn't really count until... oh, shit.

"Not exactly," Elly said, but I already knew where she was going with this. "He was involved, but it was because his picture was beside yours. Apparently, your families decided the two of you haven't been moving along quickly enough on the making things public front, so they put out an engagement announcement."

I groaned.

"Did they at least choose a flattering picture of me?" I asked.

"Not particularly. But that's not the part you should be focusing on right now," she told me.

"What else?"

"It wasn't just an engagement announcement. It was two steps short of a save the date. Evidently, you have a wedding date set for next spring."

I dropped my head against the back of the couch, the breath rushing out of me.

"Fantastic," I said. "I would really have liked to be consulted about the date of my own damn wedding."

"Are you actually going through with the wedding?" Elly asked, sounding confused.

"No, but now that the *Times* has the oh-so-romantic imagery of pictures of Preston and me beside each other, everyone's going to think I am. Everybody in New York is going to be anticipating a lavish spring wedding, and I'm going to have to explain it's not going to happen. My mother is going to be mortified when she finds out," I said.

And just like that, I started crying again. Stupid pregnancy hormones.

CHAPTER 25

NIK

There were some days when I went through so much coffee I couldn't in good conscience ask my receptionist to fill my cup every time. Considering she wasn't my assistant, it also wasn't technically part of her job. She was willing to do it for me, but that fact kept the threshold pretty low. That was one of the mornings when I used up my allotment within the first hour and a half of being in the office. It was shaping up to be a day when I definitely needed more to get me through, so I made the trek from my office to the employee break room for another refill. I tried not to think about coming here for a cup of coffee and hearing Jane swearing at the copy machine when we first came together so many months ago.

Maddie and Ethan were sitting at one of the tables, and as I filled my mug, I looked over my shoulder at them. They were sitting close together, hunched over a paper they were examining together. I swirled cream into the coffee, tasted it, and added sugar. Ethan pointed at the paper and murmured something to Maddie. Neither of them had noticed I was there. A new version of the print ad just hit the stands that week, so I assumed they were looking at it. No matter how many times we looked at the proofs of a campaign, nothing compared to actually seeing it when it was on the stands. Seeing something we designed and created in its actual context showed details in it that weren't as obvious when we were just sitting in the conference room looking at the same thing.

I hadn't gotten a chance to see the print run yet, so I carried my coffee over to the table to have a look. The sip of coffee I was taking when I got to the table stopped partway down my throat. There was a moment as I looked over Ethan's shoulder when I thought it might come back, but I forced it down painfully. He and Maddie weren't looking at anything having to do with our campaign. Staring back at me was an engagement announcement. Jane was engaged to Preston Fucking Howell. The edges of my vision turned red, and my hand tightened around the handle of my mug so hard I thought it might break.

Slamming the coffee down on the table, I reached over Ethan and snatched the paper out of his hand. Without saying a word, I whipped around and stalked out of the break room. Maddie shouted after me, but I didn't stop. I headed directly for my office and flung the door closed behind me. Locking it, I dropped the paper onto the desk and sat heavily in my chair. I pored over the announcement, taking in every detail. I read it over and over, making sure I didn't miss anything. As much as it hurt, I wanted to know everything I could find out. The announcement made my stomach turn.

Even the pictures were infuriating. Anyone with even a passing knowledge of New York society knew getting an engagement announcement in the *Times* wasn't an easy feat. The experience of trying to get the announcement of my engagement to Angela accepted by the review committee was still clear in my memory. She'd acted like it was her life's mission to have her engagement presented for all of New York society to see in the coveted weddings section of the *Times*. A photographer took pictures of us for hours, and she fussed over the proofs for even longer, selecting just the right image.

In many ways, the announcement seemed to outshine the engagement itself in her mind. That distasteful experience made looking at Jane's announcement more telling. There was no picture of them together. Instead, it was two individual pictures, completely unrelated, sitting beside each other. It told me two things. The first was that Preston and Jane's families weren't afraid to throw the clout of their names around to get perks. It fit right in with what she'd told me about the Howells and her opinion of the man she was apparently now marrying.

Seeing the two pictures beside each other also told me this man didn't come anywhere near close to deserving Jane. The lucky bastard should be sitting proudly beside her, unable to keep his hands off her. He was satisfied to throw generic pictures onto an announcement, blatantly taking such an incredible woman for granted. I couldn't take it.

This couldn't happen. There was no way I could let Jane go through with this. She didn't love this Preston guy. I knew it. It was obvious from the way she'd looked at him when I'd seen them together at dinner. It was nearly the same level of disdain she'd had when she'd told me about him in Paris. There was no way she had such a complete change of heart. I had to convince her to end this ridiculous engagement and take me back. I hadn't heard from her in six months, and no one seemed to know where she was. Even Devin, whose wife was Jane's best friend, couldn't tell me anything.

But that wasn't going to stop me. I was going to find her no matter what it took. Grabbing my phone, I called Damian, a friend from many years ago. Some men have midlife crises that convince them to buy bright red sports cars and get piercings. For Damian, his led him to a new career as a private investigator.

"Good to hear from you, Nik," Damian said when he answered the phone.

"You, too, Damian. I need you to do something for me," I said.

"What's that?"

"I need you to find someone. Her name is Jane Middlemarch," I told him.

"Middlemarch. That sounds familiar," he said.

"You probably saw her engagement announcement today," I quipped, knowing the chances of that were slim. Independently wealthy but unmarried, Damian wasn't the kind to spend his mornings perusing the weddings section.

"Why do you need me to find her?" he asked.

"Because I can't."

"I mean, is there a reason in particular you want to find her? If she's engaged..."

"Damian, I just need you to do this for me. Do whatever you need to do and send me the bill."

I ended the call and left my office.

"Sir?" my receptionist called after me. "Maddie from marketing came by asking about you."

"Tell her I'm taking the rest of the day off. Cancel my meetings."

When my driver got to the office, I climbed into the

back seat and directed him to Jane's old studio apartment. The day I found out she'd resigned, I'd gone to the building to find her and she wasn't there. A few weeks later, I tried again, but found out from a neighbor she didn't live there anymore. The rather sour old woman didn't know anything more than Jane was gone, and she'd had her belongings packed up and shipped somewhere. Now I was hoping to find out more.

After knocking on every door of the apartment building to ask where she'd gone proved fruitless, I got back in the car and sought out Jane's parents' house. It wasn't difficult to find. Her distinctive last name made researching her family easy, and soon we drove up to a gated drive in front of a sprawling home. It was far enough outside the city to seem quiet and serene, but the harsh gate kept the home from being welcoming. My driver drove up near enough to the gate for me to lean out the window and press the intercom button. A second later, a voice came through.

"Hello?"

"Hello. My name is Nik Nygard. I'm looking for Jane Middlemarch," I said.

"Miss Middlemarch isn't here," the voice said.

"Where is she?" I asked.

"I'm not at liberty to say."

The wording made my heart clench.

"Can you tell me if she has been living here with her parents?"

"No, she has not."

Frustrated, I had my driver bring me back to my house. I couldn't face going back to the office that day. There was no way I was going to be able to concentrate.

For the next two days, I searched the city for any sign of

Jane, going everywhere I could think of to find her. Finally, I heard back from Damian.

"I found her," he said. "She's in Paris."

That was all I needed to hear. I didn't need him to tell me where she was in the city. I could already see it. I knew exactly where she was. There was no hesitation. As soon as I got off the phone with Damian, I headed into my bedroom and pulled out my luggage. I threw some stuff in and headed directly for the airport, using my phone to search for a plane ticket during the ride. By the time I got there, I knew there were no commercial flights out to Paris until the next day. I wasn't willing to wait that long. I rushed to the information desk.

"How can I help you?" the woman behind the counter asked.

"I need a flight to Paris," I said.

"Of course, sir. I'm sure one of our airlines would be happy to assist you in purchasing a ticket..." she started, but I shook my head.

"No. I've already looked. There are no flights out of here until tomorrow," I told her.

"Would you like help finding accommodations for the night?" she asked, obviously confused.

"No. I'd like a private flight."

It took a few seconds for the woman's shock to wear off before she picked up her phone to arrange the flight. Less than an hour later, I climbed into a private jet and settled in for the long flight to France. With many hours in the air ahead of me, I let my mind go to when I finally arrived and found her again. I knew Jane would be in the same apartment where we'd spent the week of our business trip. It was the closest thing to home she had, far more valuable and meaningful to her than the tiny cramped place in New

York. I intended to go straight there when I arrived in Paris. Even after so many months, I remembered exactly how to get to the apartment. Nothing could fade the incredible memories of the time we'd spent together there, or the walk we took with her hand in mine.

Talking to people and going through negotiations was part of my daily life. For many years I defined my professional life with those basic techniques. Especially in my earlier days, I'd faced people far wealthier and more powerful than me, people with no interest in what I had to say. Yet I'd never felt as anxious and on edge about a meeting as I did thinking about talking to Jane again. It had to be perfect. I had to say exactly the right thing and make sure she heard it.

I rehearsed what I was going to say to her. I wanted to apologize for not telling her about Angela and explaining the situation was a mistake. And I wanted to let her know that Angela was out of my life and I wasn't interested in her. Most importantly, I wanted to make it clear that it was Jane who totally dominated my thoughts, and that she was who I loved and wanted to be with. I couldn't wait to see her again, to gather her into my arms and kiss her, to hold her, touch her, and taste her. The words churned through my mind over and over until I finally fell asleep. And when I did, it was with the peace and confidence in knowing I was going after exactly what I wanted.

I wasn't just going to Paris to confront Jane and finally say the words to her I'd been holding within me since I met her. I planned to bring her home, not just no longer engaged to Preston, but as my wife.

Marguerite was trying diligently to make sure I always had an apartment overflowing with treats and goodies, but it turned out even an adoring landlady couldn't anticipate all my cravings. All the pregnancy books I binged during my first weeks in Paris told me the cravings would subside sometime in the second trimester. So far, that was all lies. I was still having sudden waves of undeniable need for certain foods and that was what brought me out of the apartment and around the corner to the market that afternoon. A bag full of eggs, cheese, and bread balanced on my hip, ready to be turned into toads in a hole. It was something I used to eat as a child but hadn't had in years. That morning, the idea of buttery bread toasted in a pan with a fried egg in a hole in the middle sounded like the most delicious thing ever created. Nothing else stopped my hunger pangs, so off I went to the market to get the ingredients.

I reached into the bag and was nibbling on a corner of the cheese wedge when I walked through the gate into the courtyard behind the apartment building. I'd taken to using this entrance most of the time rather than going through the front door into the entryway. It felt more familiar, like I wasn't visiting the space but really living there. And the small elevator at the back of the building eliminated the need to go up the stairs, which I appreciated more and more by the day. After a particularly disturbing nightmare that involved me getting halfway up the steps, losing my sense of balance, and tipping over backward, I tried not to tempt fate. Or gravity.

It took a few steps into the courtyard for me to realize I wasn't alone. I looked up and stopped in my tracks. The bag of groceries fell from my hand and dropped to the stone pavers, broken egg streaming out onto the ground. Marguerite stood just a few yards away, smiling in her flirtatious manner as she talked to Nik, but it couldn't actually be him. After six months, he couldn't have just shown up here, but it was him. And when he turned to look at me, I could see he was just as surprised by what he saw as I was to see him.

His eyes locked on mine for an instant before sliding down my body and landing on my belly. The clingy sundress I wore was tight across my rounded stomach, exaggerating it so there was nothing to hide it. Not that I had any reason to try to. Everyone I interacted with regularly in Paris knew I was pregnant and went out of their way to pamper me and make me feel special. Nik wasn't looking at me with quite the same tenderness and excitement as the elderly couples and young artists I talked to while walking through the city. His eyes widened in surprise, but he didn't say anything. Marguerite looked back and forth between us and took her hand from where she'd rested it on his arm.

"Well, it was lovely to see you again, Nik. You are welcome anytime. I have things to tend to." She walked toward me and laid a hand affectionately on my cheek. "Jane, you will call me if you need anything, yes?"

"Yes," I told her, and she leaned in to kiss me on both cheeks before leaving the courtyard.

When the gate closed behind her, I crouched down to gather what I could salvage of the groceries, then crossed the courtyard to Nik.

"What are you doing here?" I asked.

His expression turned hard, and his shoulders pulled back.

"There are some things we need to talk about," he said.

I wanted to tell him to leave. I wanted to ask him to stay. I did neither and instead walked past him to the door to the apartment. He followed me through the back door and into the elevator. We stayed silent as the elevator rose the short distance to the back of the apartment, and we walked through the main door into the apartment itself. As soon as we stepped inside, Nik turned on me. His expression was intense, his eyes flashing with emotion.

"Preston sure works quickly," he snapped.

I narrowed my eyes on him.

"What's that supposed to mean?" I asked.

Nik gestured at me, waving his hand up and down like a frantic prize model on a game show.

"I just saw your engagement announcement, but you're already pregnant," he said.

My mouth dropped open. I stormed past him farther into the apartment, heading for the kitchen. What was he talking about? I didn't know what I was expecting when I saw him in the courtyard, but it certainly wasn't this. Nik was angry, that was clear, but was that the whole reason he got on a plane and came here? I set the bag on the kitchen counter and whirled around to face him.

"Did you come all the way to Paris to yell at me for moving on?" I asked. "Is that seriously what this is all about?" He glared at me, and I turned back around to start unloading the groceries. Three of the eggs had smashed on the courtyard stones, and I peeled the goo-covered paper wrapping away from my bread to throw it away. Tossing it out, I faced Nik again. "You know what, Nik? You don't need to worry about my pregnancy. Besides, I would think you would have far more personally pressing things to worry about right now. Like, what does your wife think about you running off to Paris to confront your former lover? Considering the way she reacted to your hotel staff not carrying her shopping bags into the inadequate penthouse, I can't imagine she is too happy about it."

Nik let out an angry breath, his nostrils flaring and his eyes glowing.

"I wouldn't know, since I don't have a wife," he said.

I rolled my eyes and shoved the remaining eggs in the refrigerator.

"Are you really going to argue semantics with me? Fine, your ex-wife," I said.

"Yes, my ex-wife. That's all she's ever going to be. Angela is gone. She has been for months."

"Elly didn't mention that to me," I pointed out.

"Maybe that's because I wasn't exactly happy about her being around in the first place and didn't broadcast the situation out to the rest of the world. I kicked her out six months ago. Then when I got to work that day, I found out you'd resigned. Maybe I should have known then," he said.

"What are you doing here, Nik? Like you said, it's been six months. Not exactly chasing me to the airport."

"I didn't know you came here. All I knew was you put in your immediate resignation and weren't going to be at the office anymore. No one knew where you went or where you were living. I went to your apartment building. I asked Devin. No one was talking," he said.

"I guess Elly is good at keeping secrets."

His eyes dropped to my belly again. "You can definitely say that."

I turned away from him to pull down one of the copper pans from the hooks that kept them organized over the kitchen island. Setting it on the stove, I turned on the burner, cranked up the heat, and put way too much butter in the pan.

"So, why now? You must not have been looking too hard for me," I said. "I told you how much I loved this place. I would have thought this would be the first place you would think of to come looking for me if you actually wanted to find me."

"According to what I knew about you, getting cut off by your parents left you with barely enough resources to pay for a shoebox apartment. Jetting off to Paris for months wasn't a possibility that crossed my mind. Of course, it didn't occur to me then that your circumstances must have changed," he said wryly.

I sliced through the crusty bread and cut holes out of the centers of the pieces before settling them into the melted butter.

"What's that supposed to mean?"

"I hated that you left and that I couldn't find you, but I figured you were going to come back eventually. Then a few days ago I saw your engagement announcement in the paper. I guess you could say it was a shock. It broke me out of my holding pattern and made me need to find you. A friend of mine who is a private investigator found you, and I came here to try to talk you out of marrying Preston. I thought I could come here and tell you what really happened with Angela and convince you not to go through with something I was sure you didn't want. But apparently, it's a futile gesture since you're already pregnant with his child."

My stomach turned and my heart clenched. Nik sounded both hurt and angry, the betrayal obvious in his eyes. This was never supposed to be this way. He wasn't supposed to find out about the baby, much less think it belonged to Preston and be so obviously hurt by it. I had to tell him the truth. I couldn't let him have come all this way only to think I was carrying Preston's child. Besides, things were different now. He was no longer my employer, and by his own admission, Angela wasn't a part of the picture. I didn't have to worry about driving a wedge between them or being a part of something I was so strongly against. This was my chance to tell Nik what he deserved to know... that he was going to be a father.

No matter what it led to for us and our future, he should have the chance to know he had a baby coming and be a part of its life. Perhaps even more than that, the baby deserved to know its father. Moving the pan off the burner, and turning off the heat, I drew in a deep breath and let it out slowly. I'd never even let myself imagine that moment. It was too painful to think about. So now I was going into it blind, unprepared for what to say or how he might react.

"Nik," I started. He stared at me from where he stood next to the island, his hand curled like it was trying to grip the marble. Maybe this wasn't the best place to have this conversation. "Come with me."

I led him out of the kitchen and into the living room. Sitting on the far end of the couch, I gestured to the other side to invite him to sit. He hesitated and crossed his arms over his chest.

"I have something to say to you. Please, sit."

He complied, sitting as far away from me as he could and keeping his hands clasped on his thighs.

"What is it?" he asked.

"This looks terrible, and I shouldn't have thought it would be better to just stay quiet. If I were you, I would think this is Preston's baby, too." I took another breath. "But it's not."

His eyes widened.

"It's not?" he asked.

I shook my head. "No, Nik. This isn't Preston's baby. It's yours."

His jaw dropped, his eyes widening even farther. His hands fell apart, and for a few seconds it looked like he was completely locked in place, like he couldn't speak. I wondered if the words had even gotten all the way into his mind or just stopped his thoughts before they processed. There was nothing I could do about it now. The truth was out there. Now it was all up to him.

The words hit me hard. I knew exactly what Jane had said, but it didn't completely process. It was like I was looking at her and hearing the words come off a TV show somewhere in the distance. The two things couldn't possibly be related. She had to have told me something else.

"What did you say?" I asked.

She tilted her head at me, then pressed her hands to the sides of her round belly.

"The baby, Nik. This baby. It's yours. It's not Preston's," she said.

That time there was no denying what she said. A wave of shock rolled over me, and I dropped back against the arm of the couch. I couldn't believe what I was hearing. The baby was mine? Even more, I couldn't believe how fast it was actually happening. This wasn't some sort of abstract concept or something to think about months into the future. This wasn't a woman announcing a pregnancy with an ultrasound picture of something that looked more like a Tic-Tac than a baby. Jane's belly was round and prominent, and every few seconds there was a little bounce, like something moving just below the surface.

Just a little more than an hour before, I didn't even know there was a baby. I was on my way from the airport, going over the plans I had in my mind for what I was going to say when I finally had Jane in front of me again. Seeing her pregnant and assuming it was Preston's child was like a punch in the gut. It made sense. Her carrying his child was the only reason I could come up with that would explain her sudden willingness to marry him after being so adamantly against it. But the thought of her being pregnant with another man's baby cut through me.

Now suddenly that had all changed. I went from not having any idea there was a baby to consider, to thinking she was going to be raising Preston's child, to realizing I was about to become a father. It was enough to send my mind reeling, and I didn't know how to respond. My eyes had drifted over to the floor, and I'd been staring at it for several seconds, just trying to get my head on straight. When I looked back over at Jane, I saw her looking back at me nervously. She chewed on her bottom lip and twisted her fingers back and forth over her belly. I'd never seen her look so unsure. It occurred to me right then I wasn't the only one still processing this news.

Telling me about the baby was a challenge for her, too. Maybe she expected me to protest, to not believe her or say it couldn't possibly be mine, but I knew that wasn't the case. She wouldn't lie to me about something like this. Even so, I did have to admit I quickly went through the math in my head, calculating how far along she would be and the last time we were together. Unless she was sleeping with Preston at the same time as me, which I highly doubted, the baby was mine. Jane was about the become the mother of my child.

She made a little gasping sound and pressed her hand to the side of her belly again. The gesture made me strangely nervous and protective, and I moved closer to her.

"What is it? What's wrong?" I asked.

She shook her head. "Nothing's wrong. The baby has hiccups. That was a particularly big one. It just feels funny sometimes."

"The hiccups? Babies can get hiccups before they're born?" I asked.

It wasn't something I'd ever considered. I didn't have any children and had never really been around anyone who did. My experiences with pregnant women were extremely limited and were never so personal as to give me insight into the baby's abilities. Jane smiled and nodded.

"Yes. This one gets them all the time. Do you want to feel?"

She reached for my hand before I had a chance to respond and pressed it against the side of her belly. Flattening her hand over it, she held it in place for a few silent seconds. At first, I didn't feel anything. Just the warmth of her skin through her tight dress. Then, there it was. A little pop against my palm. Then another. Jane giggled and I looked up at her. There was another little bounce, and I pressed my hand harder against it. I wanted to feel more. It took a few more seconds, but there it was again. My baby. Our baby.

A feeling of warmth filled me, and a smile broke out across my face. I let out a laugh, and Jane jumped, looking alarmed.

"Are you all right?" she asked.

I laughed again and nodded, hopping to my feet. "I'm more than all right. I'm far better than that. I'm fantastic."

She held up her hands to me like she was trying to calm me down.

"Maybe you should sit back down. You might be having a reaction to the long flight. Did you get any sleep?" she asked.

At that moment, I knew more than I ever had that I loved Jane. This wasn't just an infatuation. This wasn't just the intense, incredible attraction or the chemistry between us. She was the most astonishing woman I'd ever known, unexpected and wonderful in every way. How she was handling this moment just underscored it. She was worried about me, wanting to protect and take care of me. Even as she was sitting there, vulnerable and unsure of what was going to happen, she was concerned about me and how I was handling it all.

I loved Jane. Wholly and unconditionally. Irrationally and indescribably. Wanting to be with her wasn't a conclusion I was coming to because I had some sort of choice or it was a path I was deciding to go down. It was like the decision was already made for me. She was already ahead of me, already the defining feature of my future. I wasn't making that choice for myself but discovering its reality. And I never felt more alive.

Leaning down, I scooped Jane up into my arms and pulled her to her feet. I gathered her as close as her belly would allow me to and nuzzled my face into her neck. Her smell was different now, but I liked it even more. It was nothing short of intoxicating. I pulled back from the embrace and took her by her shoulders, carefully turning her around to position her standing directly in front of me.

"What are you doing?" she asked.

"I am doing something I should have done a long time ago. I should have done it that very first night when we went to dinner and you brought me back to your cramped little studio apartment," I said.

"Actually, you brought me back to my cramped little studio apartment," she pointed out. "I just walked up the stairs and didn't question it when you followed me."

"It doesn't matter who brought who or who did what. The point is, that was the first night I got to be with you, and I knew even then you were unlike anyone I'd ever encountered in my life. That night I already knew you were the woman I never wanted to let go of. So, right here, right now, I'm going to do what I should have done then," I told her.

This was it. There was no pomp and circumstance. No choreographed drama or overdone atmosphere to make the mood seem romantic. There were no theatrics. This moment wasn't ever going to grace the big screen or become a fairy-tale feature in a magazine, but it was perfect. It was our moment.

I got down on one knee in front of Jane and reached out to take her hand in mine.

"Nik," she breathed, her eyes widening slightly.

"When I saw that engagement announcement, it shattered me, Jane. I couldn't let you go. I didn't care what it took, I was going to find you and bring you home. I got onto that flight so fast, I didn't even have the chance to prepare. So, here I am, without a ring. I don't have anything to put on your finger right now. But—" I reached into my pocket and pulled out my wallet. Taking hold of the corner of my credit card, I shook it free so the rest of the wallet fell to the floor, then placed it in her palm. "Here. It's not exactly the same, but I want you to see this as a promise. This symbolizes my promise to get you the most magnificent ring the moment I have the chance. I will pick it out for you and surprise you with it, or you can come with me and choose whatever you want yourself, but I will get you the ring you deserve."

Jane looked at me like I was crazy, and she still wasn't completely sure I knew what I was doing. But it didn't stop me. I held her hand tighter and kept going.

"Jane, I have loved you for so long now. I think I started falling in love with you the first second you walked into the office after I saw your sketches. I was definitely falling in love with you by the time I found you going to battle against the copy machine and losing miserably. And I know I loved you when we got to Paris. I have loved you every day since, but nowhere near as much as I love you now. I should have told you earlier. You are everything I need and everything I never knew I wanted. I promise I will be there for you, and I will be there for our baby. I will take care of both of you and make time for both of you. We will build a family together, and it will be the center of my world. If you will let me. So, please, Jane, will you marry me?"

"Will you marry me?"

I stood there staring at Nik down on his knee in front of me and didn't know how to react. I didn't know what to think or say. It was all happening so fast, and I never could have expected it. Did he really just tell me he loved me? Could it possibly be true he not only loved me in that moment, but that he always had, just the way I had always loved him? When did all this happen?

And, more importantly, why was I standing here holding his credit card?

I looked into his eyes. They stared back at me with hope and anticipation. In all the months I'd known him, I'd tried to understand the emotion in those eyes. Open and blue, they were like staring into the purest ocean, but just like the ocean, they hid everything just beneath the surface. There were times when it seemed impossible to figure out what he was thinking or feeling. Even in the moments I was pretty certain I knew what was going through his mind, his eyes could make me question it. But not at that moment. Looking into his eyes as he stared at me, I could see the sincerity and longing I hoped for. This just wasn't what I could have ever envisioned.

"Did you seriously just propose to me with your credit card?" I asked, holding up the black card.

He looked at it for a few seconds, like he was letting the reality of the decision churn through the gears of his mind.

"I told you, I was in so much of a hurry to get here I didn't think about buying a ring. But I promise you'll have the most incredible engagement ring you can imagine just as soon as we can find it," Nik said.

"I can understand you rushing out of New York so fast you didn't get a ring, but you're in Paris. You could have stopped at one of the countless stands on the sidewalk and gotten me a flower?" I asked. "You've seen *Beauty and the Beast*, right? There are roses literally all over the place in France."

I swirled my hand around in front of him like I was encompassing the entirety of the country. Nik looked like he was going to say something, and then his mouth closed.

"Um," he said a few seconds later.

I tried to keep a straight face but couldn't. I laughed and held the card out to him.

"Put this away," I told him. When the card was securely back in his wallet and his wallet sitting on the coffee table, I pulled him to his feet. "I don't need your credit card. I don't need the promise of an expensive, elaborate engagement ring. You don't need to put a down payment on our future together for me to want you, Nik. I just need to know you love me and want us to be together."

He took my hands in his, bringing them up to his chest to hold them over his heart.

"I know that wasn't the most romantic proposal that has

ever happened, but I want you to know I meant every word of it. And so many more I haven't even figured out yet. But I'll keep trying. I'll spend the rest of my life just trying to find all the words that exist that will tell you how I feel about you and what you mean to me. If you'll let me." He released my hands and brought his up to cup my face, leaning forward to rest his forehead against mine. "These months without you have been agony. I feel like I haven't even been living. I've just been going day by day, trying to get by. Waiting to wake back up and be alive again."

I wrapped my hands around his wrists and drew in a breath of him. My eyes closed and I leaned against him, just wanting to feel the warmth and strength of Nik near me again.

"I know exactly what you mean. That's what I've felt like, too. Even being here has felt less magical because I didn't have you here beside me to experience it all with me. I have missed you so much. More than I could ever tell you," I whispered.

"You'll never have to miss me like that again. I won't spend another minute without you. You've always been mine, Jane. Always. From the very beginning, we were linked, and there's no way I'm willing to spend any more of my life wondering what it could be like to spend it with you," he said.

A tear ran down my cheek, and I opened my eyes to look at Nik again. I stepped slightly back from him so I could see him fully. It had been so long since I was just able to look at him this way. I wanted to take him in, to fill every sense with him.

"It was all so much. I wasn't sure what to do when I found out about the baby. By the time I found out, I'd already seen you with Angela, and then she moved into your house, and you wouldn't talk to me or tell me what was going on," I told him.

Nik shook his head, lowering our hands and guiding me over to sit back down on the couch with him.

"That was a serious mistake. I never should have tried to keep you separated from it," he said.

"Why did you? Why didn't you just tell me what was going on?" I asked.

"Because I wanted to protect you. Because I didn't want you to find out about the mistakes of my past or be dissuaded by seeing the remnants of my broken relationship. I was afraid if I let you too close to Angela and started overlapping those two parts of my life, you would not like what you saw and run away from me," he explained.

"It's not two parts of your life," I said. "It's just your life. I'm well aware you had one before I walked into it, just like I did. It doesn't mean I'm going to take what happened to you then as the gospel truth of what will happen moving forward. What I care about is here and now. Us together. It scared me so much when I saw the two of you sitting there together, then found out she was moving back in with you. I couldn't understand that, and you not saying anything to me just made it worse. It was like I was all fun and games to you when we were away on business, but then she came in and you went back to real life again. There's no way I could compete with that."

"You're right," Nik said. "You couldn't compete with that." The words made the breath catch in my throat and my heart ache, but he leaned closer to me. "Because there's no competition. Angela is my ex-wife. Nothing more. And she never will be anything more. When she came to me and told me her husband left her and she had nothing, I felt guilty. You might not understand that, but even though I didn't want to be with her when we divorced and definitely don't want to be with her now, I still carry the guilt that I hurt another person with my own selfishness and bad decisions. Even that wasn't enough to make me want to have her back as part of my life. I only intended on her staying in the penthouse for a few days while she decided what she was going to do next. I was getting ready to tell her to leave, and she knew it. That's why that day when we were in the conference room and she came in, she did what she does best. She lied and manipulated."

"What do you mean?" I asked.

I listened while Nik told me about Angela's disgusting deception. It infuriated me to think of her putting him through that. It was worse to know he went through it alone. I held his hands tightly and looked intently into his eyes.

"You have nothing to feel bad about," I said. "You are a good man, a far better person than she deserved to have in her life at all, much less during that time. I could never blame you for that. I was just so confused when I found out I was pregnant. We hadn't decided what we were to each other, and I didn't want to tell you about the baby if you were trying to reconcile with your wife. That's not the kind of life I would ever want to have. I thought that if I told you and you left her for me, I'd have felt forever like the only reason you were with me is because of the baby and not because you really wanted to be."

"But what about Preston? What was that all about?" Nik asked.

"I honestly didn't know what to do. I knew I couldn't just keep working at the office and pretend nothing was going on. Eventually I was going to start showing and you were going to piece things together. Then Preston called me. He said his parents were still on his back, and even though he didn't want to marry me either, he thought we could benefit from each other. He suggested a marriage of convenience to appease our parents and give us a leg up in society. I didn't care so much about what society thought of me being in my late twenties and not married, but I did care about not knowing what was going to happen in my future. I decided to agree to his proposition to buy me some time to figure out what to do. It bought me some comfort while I pieced together what life was going to look like now that I was about to be out of a job and a mother," I explained.

"That night when I saw the two of you together at the restaurant, is that when he asked you?" Nik asked.

I nodded. "Yes. I hadn't given him an answer yet."

"I wish I had known."

"So do I."

"Did you tell him about the baby?" he asked.

"No. I still haven't. I came here the day after I resigned and haven't been back home since. That engagement announcement came as just as much of a shock to me as it did to everyone else," I told him.

"I wish I had been open with you about everything that was going on so you would have felt like you could come to me about this. There was never even a single second of interest in reconciling with Angela. She thought there was, but I shut that down as soon as she tried."

"You did?"

"Yes. I told her in no uncertain terms there was nothing between us and never would be anything between us. I told her there was someone else I wanted to be with." He brushed the tip of his nose against mine. "You are the only woman I want, Jane. The only woman I can't stop thinking about. You are the woman I can't wait to have a family with."

Nik's hand ran over my belly, and my heart nearly burst. This was everything I had dreamed of but wouldn't allow myself to think about. It seemed impossible, like I could never have this dream, but it was right in front of me, now. He leaned forward and I met his mouth in a kiss. It was soft and gentle at first, almost cautious, like we were testing the waters of each other after so long apart. But very quickly we realized it was all still there. We still knew each other, understood each other.

His mouth pressed more fully against mine, and his lips parted to deepen the kiss. The tip of his tongue dipped into my mouth and swept across my tongue, igniting desire inside me. My body awakened at the taste of him, and the trace of his fingertips along the straps of my dress over my shoulders was enough to send electricity to the tips of my fingers and the ends of my toes. I moaned into the kiss, and Nik drew me closer to him. He pulled the straps of my dress down my arms, then led the top down off my breasts until it reached my waist. I lay back against the arm of the couch so he could take off my sandals, then slip the rest of the clingy fabric off.

He didn't hesitate to slip my panties off and toss them away. It felt so natural being this way with him. I was bare and uninhibited, not wanting to hide anything from him. Nik gazed at me, his eyes roving over me with reverence, admiration, and love. Never in my life had I felt so beautiful as I did in that moment.

Reaching forward, Nik ran his fingertips over my breasts. More sensitive now, they tingled at the gentle brush of my skin, and my nipples tightened. He traced his touch down the sides of my rib cage and into the dip of my waist, coming to my hips. For a moment he held on to them, applying gentle pressure, then he stood and reached for my hands. He walked backward through the apartment, remembering every step that brought us to the bedrooms. The door to the one I was using stood open, and he led me through it, scooping me up to cradle me in his arms as soon as I was inside.

He carried me over to the bed, and the memory of him tossing me onto the mattress sprang into my mind. But he didn't do that again. This time, he lowered me down carefully, draping me across the comforter and resting my head on the pillow. As I watched him, he undressed. The sight of his exceptional body made mine even more ready for him, and I ached to touch him. Finally, he climbed onto the bed and settled beside me, resting on one arm and propping himself up on his elbow. He stared down into my face as he brought his hand to my body again.

It ran down the side of my face along my jawline, then down the side of my neck and onto my breast. My stomach fluttered and my skin tingled as he traced a line down the center of my body and finally found the wet heat between my thighs. His fingertips slid through my folds and rediscovered every sensitive inch. I gasped at the new intensity, overcome with physical pleasure and powerful emotions that swept through me as he reintroduced my body to his touch.

Within seconds I couldn't stand not touching him for a single further instant. I tucked my hand beneath his arm and ran it along his belly until I found his hard shaft. Wrapping my hand around it, I picked up his rhythm, stroking him just as his fingers played across me.

CHAPTER 29

NIK

Jane's hand felt warm and soft around my shaft. I groaned, my body instantly responding to the familiar, delirious touch. I'd been dreaming of that touch for eight months since the last time we were there in Paris and I had Jane naked and in my arms. It fulfilled me, soothing a deep ache and taking the edge off the anxiety that settled into my bones when I went days and weeks and months without feeling her skin.

I leaned over to kiss her, and our bodies explored and worshipped each other, expressing through the pleasure everything we wanted to tell each other. The words we could say to each other were one thing. But this was something else. It transcended those words and what they meant. Anyone could say those same words, but only we could create the magic between us.

After a few minutes of gradually, patiently warming each other up, I rested my hand to Jane's hip and carefully turned her over onto her side. I curled my body around hers so she molded into me. I fully enveloped her, my body stretching above hers, so her head rested on the front of my shoulder, and beneath so our feet intertwined. She supported her head with one arm, and I wrapped my arm over her head to hold her hand. The other hand stayed on her hip, supporting me as I pressed my hips forward to nudge my erection into the warmth between her thighs. She let out a soft moan and closed her eyes, arching her back just slightly so she opened up to me.

I ran my hand down her thigh and tucked it between her knees to lift it slightly. It allowed me to sink inside her, bonding our bodies. I held her close and rocked into her. There was no hurry, no urgency or rush. I just wanted to feel her. It was only us now, and we had all the time in existence. No one would keep us apart again. Not now and not ever. This was the woman I wanted to spend the rest of my life with, and I couldn't wait to see what every day of that life would hold.

When it was over and our bodies were warm, relaxed, and satisfied, I held Jane close to me and just savored the way her skin felt against mine. I thought I knew what she felt like and really experienced her the other times we were together, but as I lay there, listening to the softness of her breath and stroking the sweat from her skin, I knew I hadn't. There was no way for me to know that then, of course. It was only in thinking I'd lost her, in being forced to be away from her, that I realized just how much more I could appreciate her.

And that's exactly what I did as we lay there. I ignored everything else. Nothing mattered but her. Without any focus on anything else, I could devote my senses fully to her. I breathed in the smell of her and identified everything that went into the sweet, musky, heady mix. The freshness of her shampoo, soap still clinging to her skin, her sweat, her arousal. I listened to the sound of her breath, then rested my head against the side of her neck and heard her heartbeat drumming just beneath her skin. I kissed the back of her shoulder and swept the tip of my tongue across it, tasting salt. I concentrated on the very tips of my fingers and how they each took in the texture of her skin.

She was everything. I didn't need anything else in those moments. She was the air I breathed, and she nourished me. As I lay there holding her, I knew I had reached a new level. I had never felt happier or more complete than I did at that moment. Just like I told her, Jane was everything I ever wanted, even if I didn't know it. That's when I realized I'd spent my entire life not even really knowing what I most needed. I thought I did. I thought I had everything figured out and was doing everything I could to pursue my greatest happiness. I didn't know the thing that would bring me my greatest joy and fulfill me like no other wasn't even something I knew about. Well before I met her, well before I had any concept of her, Jane was already in my heart. She was part of my soul.

Life couldn't get any better than this. As soon as that thought went through my mind, I knew it wasn't true. My hand slipped onto her belly and gently stroked over it. That was where it was going to get better. Soon, we were going to have a child, and that would make life richer and sweeter than either of us could even imagine.

It was hard to wrap my head around the reality that just beneath my hand was my child. I knew the baby was there. I could see the full, rounded swell of Jane's belly and had felt the shifting and bouncing of the baby's hiccups, but it was still such an extraordinary concept. It was right there, a child we'd created together, and before long, it would be born into this world. Life would never be the same. From the moment she told me, I was a father. The baby may still be waiting to be born, but it was my child and I was its father. The world was different. Every decision I ever made was different. Every plan for the future, every thought I ever had, every belief, question, and idea, it all rushed around in my head, going through this new filter.

I was thinking about this family, and this child. I was looking ahead just a few short weeks to an entirely different chapter. It was exciting. Enough of my life had already been devoted to building an empire. It was time to build a family that would put a reason behind all that hard work. The power and wealth I accumulated was no longer just about me. It would give Jane and our child the kind of life they deserved, and one day I would pass it along. It was a legacy I could give to this baby and it could then build and pass along. The thoughts kept flowing through my mind, turning to dreams as I fell asleep.

The next morning, I got out of bed carefully so I wouldn't wake Jane. She'd slept so comfortably throughout the night, and I didn't want to disturb her. She needed the rest. I wanted her to stay healthy and get as much sleep as she could before the baby came. I slipped out of the apartment and walked down the narrow cobblestone street until I got to one of the larger main streets. It didn't take me long to find what I was looking for, and I was back at the apartment in less than half an hour.

Making sure Jane slept enough was a priority, but I also wanted to make sure she was eating well to keep both of them strong. She woke up after a few hours' nap the afternoon before and finished the dinner she was craving, but it didn't seem like enough. I went to work making her breakfast, intending to bring it into the bedroom for her.

Rich smells of eggs, bacon, and buttered bread filled the apartment. I set two laden plates on a tray and added glasses of juice before carrying it back to the bedroom. Jane was just waking up as I walked into the room, and she smiled when she saw me holding the tray. She pulled herself up to sitting and tucked several pillows behind her. I settled the tray into her lap, and her smile widened when she looked down at it.

She picked up the rose I bought for her that morning from the vendor on the sidewalk. Bringing it close to her face, she closed her eyes as she breathed in the smell. Her eyes moved back over to me.

"You brought me a flower," she said softly.

"Well, they are all over France," I teased.

Sitting down beside her, I took one of the plates and a fork. We ate in silence for a few seconds, before she looked at me.

"Thank you for coming for me," she said.

I ran the backs of my fingers along the side of her face.

"I couldn't help myself," I told her. "I love you, Jane."

Her eyes grew misty, but a smile curved her lips.

"I love you, too, Nik," she said.

My chest felt like it was going to burst my heart swelled so much at hearing those words. I knew I'd never get enough of it. There was nothing quite like hearing her voice tell me she loved me, and I intended to make sure I heard it many, many more times.

"You know," I said, taking a bite of bacon. "You never did give me an answer to my question."

"Oh?" Jane said, mimicking innocence. She took a sip of

juice and picked up her fork again to take another bite of eggs. "I didn't?"

"No," I said with a laugh, "you didn't."

"Then I guess you're just going to have to ask me again."

I leaned in toward her.

"This time without the credit card?" I asked in a lowered tone.

She leaned toward me.

"That would probably be for the best," she whispered.

I set my plate aside and took her hand.

"Jane Middlemarch, will you marry me?" I asked.

She grinned. "Yes. I would love to marry you."

I kissed her, then dipped my head to kiss her belly.

"Well, I'm glad we got that formality taken care of now," I said, going back to my breakfast.

"Why is that?" she asked suspiciously.

"Because I want to get married here, in Paris. Before we go back to New York," I told her matter-of-factly.

Jane laughed. "You've lost your mind."

She ate another bite of her breakfast, shaking her head slightly as if she thought I'd backpedal, but I didn't.

"That might be true but waiting to make you mine will drive me even crazier. I need to marry you as soon as possible," I said.

She stared at me for a few seconds, then shrugged.

"It has always been my dream to get married in Paris," she admitted.

I smiled happily.

"Then that will be the first of your dreams I will fulfill for you. Then I will make it my life's work to fulfill the rest of them."

"There's just one thing," Jane said.

"What's that?" I asked. "Anything. You tell me, and I will make it so."

"Do you think we can get the *Times* to print a retraction?"

I laughed and gathered her up in another kiss. She would never stop amazing me.

EPILOGUE

JANE - ONE YEAR LATER...

I bent over the worktable in my office, looking closely over some stills from the latest photoshoot. I frowned and tilted my head, getting a slightly different angle. The images looked good, but not exactly what I thought they were going to look like. The vibe wasn't quite there. Something was missing. My back ached from my hunched position, and I straightened, arching backward to stretch the muscles. I thought having standing desks and not sitting down to work all day was supposed to be better. It might be making me more productive, but I hadn't quite gotten the hang of working standing up without the day ending in a stiff back.

I glanced at the clock over the door and was shocked by how late it had gotten. Spending two hours bent over in the same position looking at the pictures was probably more the culprit behind the backache than the standing itself. Mystery solved, but that wasn't my biggest concern at that moment. My daughter would be getting hungry soon, and I hadn't stopped to get her lunch ready for her. Almost as soon as the thought went through my head, a cry rose up from the playpen positioned on the wall behind my table and that baby was like clockwork. You could time a train by her crying for her feedings. She got that from her father. I walked around the desk and leaned into the playpen to scoop my baby girl up. Cradling her against my chest, I snuggled her and nuzzled my face into the side of her chubby little neck.

"Come on, sweet Rose. We'll go get something to eat," I murmured to her.

I headed to the break room where an entire shelf in the fridge was dedicated to bottles of pumped breastmilk. The walk too much longer now than it had in my days before Rose. In those days I could just scurry down the hall from the marketing department, grab a snack or a cup of coffee, and be back at my desk in less than five minutes. Now I had to plan for all the extra time it would take just to make it past the other offices and desks.

Not that I minded. It was fun having everyone coo and fuss over the baby. It wasn't like they could help it. She was adorable. I was happy to be able to have her there with me while I was working and not have to leave her at a daycare or with a sitter, but that would have been far too hard. Having her in the office meant Rose had us close by all the time, and we could enjoy every moment of parenting her. Even if it was fairly unconventional for part of my office to be set up as a nursery.

I was pretty sure the promotion I landed a few months before had something to do with the extra perk. After the campaign we shot in Paris more than a year and a half ago experienced tremendous success that created momentum for a year of exceptional marketing, Devin offered Ethan a spot at one of his own companies. Toby and Nik gave him their blessing, and he took the job, paving the way for Maddie to move up to the director of marketing. And that left her position as assistant director open and, just like a domino, I fell right into it.

Then again, the fact that my husband and the father of the sweet baby taking up residence in my office was one of the owners of the company probably didn't hurt matters. Immediately after Nik and I got married, I made it very clear to him the marriage wasn't going to derail me. Now that I had experienced the rush of having my own career and building it based on something I was proud of and good at, I didn't want to let it go. I wanted to be a good wife and mother but wasn't willing to just give up what I'd worked so hard for.

That campaign put the brand on the map, and each one after had only increased the popularity and success of the company. Within just a few months of the full launch, the app was one of the most downloaded in the world. Demand for further developments got stronger every day. Things were going truly fantastically for me in my career, and I was proud of it. Nik could have completely supported me and let me go right into the life of a pampered, spoiled house-wife people always assumed I would be. And maybe there would be a time when I let that happen. But for right then, I was enjoying my career far too much. Since I wasn't willing to not work and I also wasn't willing to have someone else raising my baby, the compromise we came to was having Rose with me in the office every day. It was working out perfectly.

Except at that particular moment things weren't

working out perfectly for the baby. She had apparently gotten especially hungry during that last nap and was crying again. Her little body tensed up, and she balled her fists in frustration. At not quite eleven months old, Rose wasn't really talking yet. She had a few words she was able to say, but for the most part it was just babbling and trying to figure things out. There were times when I could see just how frustrated she got with not being able to communicate in any way other than crying, and it broke my heart.

"Just a few more seconds, baby," I cooed to her. "We're almost there."

She buried her head into my shoulder, and I hurried the rest of the way to the break room.

"I think I should start having donuts delivered in the afternoon. There's usually a box of them sitting in here in the morning, but a couple hours after lunch is really when people need to perk up."

I heard Nik's voice before I saw him. Rose did, too, and her little head lifted from my shoulder. She immediately stopped crying and perked up, her big blue eyes flashing around the room looking for her daddy. A second later he came around the side of the small eating area and saw us. His face lit up in a bright smile, and he opened his arms out to us.

"Hey! There are my girls. This is definitely the best thing I've ever found in the break room," he said, stepping up to me and leaning in for a kiss.

"Are you discussing the finer points of having donuts in the break room in the afternoon?" I asked.

"Yes, I am," he confirmed. He scooped Rose out of my arms and held her up over his head, twirling her around until she giggled in delight, her hunger apparently forgotten for the moment. "Because donuts are delicious, and they make people happy."

He said that last part right to the baby, lowering his voice like it was a secret conspiracy just between the two of them to bring the joy of fried dough, icing, and sprinkles to the world at large.

"It's good to see you working hard," I teased. I reached up to tickle Rose's tummy. "Right now, this one is feeling a bit hungry. But since the donut extravaganza hasn't begun, I'm going to go ahead and warm up a bottle for her."

I went to the refrigerator to get the bottle while Nik continued to dote on Rose. While the bottle warmed in the microwave, I watched the two of them together. There was nothing more beautiful, nothing that made my heart glow, like seeing Nik and Rose with each other. I took the bottle from the microwave and shook it, dribbling some on my wrist to make sure it wasn't too hot. When I was satisfied it was perfect, I brought it back over to Nik. Without question, he took the bottle from my hand and tipped Rose back in his arms so he could feed her.

He was an amazing father. There were days when he came into my office to take the baby and brought her around with him while he had meetings and checked on each of the departments. There was never a second's hesitation when she needed to be changed, and over the last couple of months, he had been patiently holding her tiny hands and helping her pull up to her feet to learn to walk.

Rose was only a few months old when Nik started saying he wanted to expand our family. Over the last couple of months, that conversation turned to him saying he was ready and wanted to talk about having another baby in the near future. I wasn't so sure at first. My bond with Rose had been instant and incredible, and for a long time I couldn't imagine having anyone else be a part of our lives. Recently, that had changed, and now I knew I definitely wanted the same thing. With such a devoted and hands-on partner in Nik, I was ready to have another child. The thought was thrilling. I couldn't wait to see Rose playing with her little brother or sister, and the doubled joy of watching Nik with our children.

I stood close beside Nik and leaned against his arm to watch him feed Rose. He leaned down to whisper in my ear.

"I have a surprise for you tonight."

"You do? What is it?" I asked.

"If I tell you, it won't be much of a surprise, will it?" he asked.

"Actually, yes. Yes, it will. It will just be a surprise right now rather than later," I pointed out.

"All right. Fair enough. I'll tell you. In honor of our upcoming first anniversary, we are going on a trip. To Paris," he told me.

I gasped. "Paris? It's been months."

"I know, but we will make it our new tradition. I've already got everything packed. All we have to do is head to the airport. The private jet will be waiting for us. And by now I'm sure Marguerite has already started filling the apartment with food for you. I'm going to talk to her again about buying the place," he told me.

"You know she won't let you. How is she supposed to dote on us and know everything about our lives if she isn't renting the apartment to us a few times a year?" I asked with a laugh. "But don't worry, when I was twenty, she promised to leave it to me in her will."

Nik laughed and I kissed him, my heart filled with love. Everything in my life was perfect, and it was all thanks to the incredible man I loved. I truly did have to be willing to lose everything to gain the life of my dreams.

The End

www.ingramcontent.com/pod-product-compliance
Lightning Source LLC
Chambersburg PA
CBHW020332160726
47992CB00004B/1809